AFRICAN WRITERS SERIES

FOUNDING EDITOR   Chinua Achebe

AFRICAN WRITERS SERIES

241

The Slums

THOMAS AKARE

The Slums

HEINEMANN

Heinemann International
a division of Heinemann Educational Books Ltd
Halley Court, Jordan Hill, Oxford OX2 8EJ

Heinemann Educational Books Inc
361 Hanover Street, Portsmouth, New Hampshire, 03801, USA

Heinemann Educational Books (Nigeria) Ltd
PMB 5205, Ibadan
Heinemann Kenya Ltd
PO Box 45314, Nairobi, Kenya
Heinemann Educational Boleswa
PO Box 10103, Village Post Office, Gaborone, Botswana
Heinemann Publishers (Caribbean) Ltd
175 Mountain View Avenue, Kingston 6, Jamaica

LONDON   EDINBURGH   MELBOURNE   SYDNEY
AUCKLAND   SINGAPORE   MADRID
HARARE   ATHENS   BOLOGNA

ISBN 0 435 90241 5

Set in 10pt. Plantin
by Elanders Ltd, Corby, Northants
Printed and bound in Great Britain by
Cox & Wyman Ltd, Reading, Berkshire

90   91   92   93   94   95   10   9   8   7   6   5   4   3

For
Halima and Saada
and for
Fauziya (Ju-Ju), Asha and Juma,
my children, whose lives will not, I hope,
be like those of the Slums people

In memory of
Mzee Agustino Mulo Opondo,
my father

1

The bell tolled and its echo kept ringing into my ears for some time before fading away. I sat. Dong, dong, dong, it repeated again. I kept sitting under this statue of Queen Mary holding her young infant son, Jesus, in her arms. I watched them. The people. Disappearing into the church. I knew why. And what they were going to do. It was Sunday morning and yesterday was Saturday. They were going to pray in the Mass as they were Catholics . . . I mean Christians. I'm a Christian too, with a Christian name, but a funny thing: I couldn't go into the church, or I never went. I'm somehow ashamed or something, I don't know what. I think I know why. It made me swear: 'On myself and the Satan of my arse, I will never attend church again.'

I kept on sitting there, I don't know for how long, only that I knew now that this bell tolling was the second time, indicating that the Mass going on was the second one. I supported my chin with both my hands, and somehow I was feeling cold. Last night our sleep was not good in the Slums in those wrecks of taxi cars which to us are our homes.

I looked up at the Queen Mary Mother of Jesus with her son in her arms. I thought about the love and tenderness that this statue of a nut had. The tenderness I had so many years back when I was a baby boy. The time I never knew what it was to suffer, or what life was. A little cry and mama and dad would demand to know what was amiss. I was cared for. But now if I opened my mouth to cry I wonder what people would think of me. I would look a silly bastard. I think they would try to penetrate, focusing their eyes deep into my throat to see what was inside. I would look a crazy fool. I'm a big lost poor son in a big world.

And as they are out-of-date cars they could not keep out the cold

1

or the warmth. And as the night was chilly it was the worse. The back seat, my bed, had started to wear off. I mean the cover. So the springs were not very welcoming to any visitors, apart from me and Hussein. Luckily no visitors came along. That skeleton of a car must have given the owner a wonderful time on the road. It was a Zephyr and white cream in colour. Its tyres were worn out and it was only recently that we supported it with blocks of stone to balance it. And its windows too were broken. Anyway it was our home. It supplied us with a shelter at night.

Last night was really cold, and as my clothing was on its last voyage on earth I could not sleep a wink. And to make the matter worse the police were very disturbing. Especially to people like us who have no proper homes. They, the police, were doing the msako, the vagrants' inspection for the unemployed and the tax-defaulters who don't pay up their GPTs. They were to be rounded up and returned to their rural areas. They are a nuisance to the government. Thieves with no profit to the law. We were worried, so that to sleep was a task. But luck was with us, because they didn't bother to come to our homes, or perhaps they came and found nobody. We escaped. Ran away from the law. Each sought out his refuge on his own. As for me, I walked the whole night out and came to rest outside the night-clubs on this Racecourse Road. I blew the night outside Molo Club. I left there for this place under the statue.

I kept on sitting, looking at these people going into the church, others going to their businesses and some going, where to they didn't know, trying to escape the world's trouble. I thought and wondered to myself, why doesn't the government want us? Why charge us for vagrancy in our country, unemployed or tax-defaulters, while it is not our wish or our fault? We don't eat their food or beg. As for education, we have that, but no jobs. What crime is that? And it is all due to corruption and tribalism, nepotism. Why send us back to the land where today is the same as yesterday, and so is every year. Then I found myself having a feeling of hatred watching these people and all their commotion. The feeling was so deep that I felt myself envying them. I looked at them with envious eyes when I thought where they had slept, what food they

2

ate and the way they were dressed. The mumbo-jumbo fashions. Suits, minis, maxis, bell-bottoms and flares, slim-fit shirts and all.

I hated their clothing and the way they looked in it. Very smart indeed. I looked at my hands. Not very dirty, because every day we were in contact with water. Perhaps they were the cleanest parts of my body, followed by the eyes.

The rest of the body was nothing but a covering of dirt. To have a bath in the Slums you have to line up in the toilets or else lick the dirt or scratch it off. I looked at my jacket. The patch which I had sewn there had started to wear out. I cursed this sack thread. It couldn't hold for long. I needed another two patches on the shoulders. My blue Lee trousers also needed one on the bottom, right up to between my thighs. My last Y-front was almost worn to a thread in the centre and to add to it I saw three lice along the strap. They had started laying the eggs of their young. I thought I would throw it away with the lice, because I didn't kill them when I saw them. They too had to make a living, but worst of all they depended on my blood. It would be upon them because they had sucked me long enough. I coiled my toes in the boots. My socks were like football ankle-caps. My safari boots were no different from a guy walking barefoot. They swallowed dust like their mother. These thoughts added to my hatred when I observed these people in front of me. Then a thought struck me. Was I this way because I never entered the church and worse because I'm a Christian? This thought intrigued me and made me admit that I'm really a sinner.

I was about to stand up and go into the church when again I remembered something I read somewhere, I don't know in which magazine or paper, but I found myself smiling at that thought. It read: On Sunday mornings, some people go to churches to pray for the success of the seeds they planted last night and some for them to fail. Then I knew I was not the only sinner, no more than those who were now pretending to show the others their faith, in good clothing. After this I thought of my lunch money and decided to go back to Katanga Base in the Slums. My return journey to Katanga Base was not a long one.

3

I hurried from St Peter's church along the Racecourse taking this Pumwani Road and following it to Gikomba. Along this road were many people moving to town and others moving back. Some stood lazily with nowhere to go to, some looked at passers-by with those eyes full of changaa and muratina hangovers. Too red. Under the bridge beside the river a man was bathing. He had no care. A woman, mother of three, was busy cooking the noon lunch. The food was nothing but irio: comprising vegetables, beans, maize and potatoes. Her youngest hanging on her back with a face that hadn't been washed since yesterday morning with traces of dried porridge running from mouth to ears and downwards to the chin and on to the chest. The rest of the family played around just near with the other family too. Also near the kiosk I noticed a small used-up Peugeot pick-up van covered up with some rugs, mainly sacks and worn out old blankets and plastic papers. That was the family home. I hated it, comparing it to ours. In ours you had no room to stretch your legs and we were sharing it too, I, Eddy, and my friend Hussein. I envied that woman.

Apart from her kiosk were others selling tea, sambusa, mandazi and porridge. Besides them the bus garage, timber-yard and this famous Bombay furniture place which dealt mostly with coffins and displayed them just outside here. They reminded people of their last day.

I kept on moving when this bus moved past blowing its diesel smoke and dust on us and hooting its trumpet-like horn. I cursed him and wished the most odd things to happen to him. I came to a stop at this petrol station where there were some buses of the same make as the one which blew dust on us. It looked like their terminus. Here people were welcoming their relatives and families. Most of them from Western. Here I stopped a bit to watch the scene. Then I read the inscriptions on these buses. They read: 'Family Service Company', with J.J.J. before them. I counted the number of them and reached seven, all painted blue and yellow, Leyland models. I thought to myself wondering how many people were joint partners in that business. Then suddenly a black Mercedes-Benz rolled to a stop. Out came this short man in an Italian business suit, black. He appeared to me a man with no care

4

in this suffering world. A man with quids, I mean. He was brown and not so old. He must have been around thirty-five or forty. On his face was an inch-long scar. It must have come from a panga blow or a knife. Or even a bottle, who knows. He inspected the parking of his car and nodded, smiling internally. He tucked his shirt in and tightened up his trousers. After this drum beating started from somewhere, some drums with deep sounds and some with light ones. They made the tune sound good. I looked around a bit before I saw them. Both men and women. Young and old. And all in white. The men had on kabutis and white turbans. Black singhs, I thought. The women had on white long dresses to their knees and down to their ankles; some wore Akalla shoes while others had none, their feet all covered with brown dust. This was a proof that they must have come from up country. In town here you don't find that type of dust. They accompanied the drum-beats with their voices. Man, those people could really sing. I thought they could be very good in high pitches. But one or two had flat tones. They must have perhaps have spent the whole night practising. Sweat started pouring out on their faces. That song seemed to have no end as I listened to it. Then this man joined them. He too sang. Man, that did it. Those people went wild. The sound went up. I watched them forgetting all about going to Katanga Base. Then I heard someone behind me telling his friend: That guy, meaning the Benz man, is the owner of these buses.

And these people singing, who are they? asked the other. They are Akorino, he answered. That sect of convertees saved from sins.

But don't they have a church? asked the other.

No, they don't. They are invited here by this man, as he is one of them. He needs some blessings on his buses to keep them from accident, and do you know something? He is not all that educated. He can't even write.

So at last I came to know the owner of those buses. I had seen them often but I never knew who the damn hell the owner was. Then the education part stung my heart. A thing that I didn't like hearing of. It always reminded me of my troubles during school time, how we used to be deceived about what we would be after

5

school and how we would enjoy life. All crap. It made me envy that guy. If he didn't attend school and he was worth all that, then there is no need to go to school, or university. Then I started asking myself how did he get started? And where did he get the money from? With this thought I decided to move on to Katanga Base. On my way I bought a ten-cent piece of maize with my last penny that I had tied in a knot in my hankie.

The time was getting near noon when I reached Katanga. I found my fellow boys busy washing cars. I looked around to see if I could see any of my customers. I saw none of them. I stood and watched my friends, envying them for what they would get while I got nothing. Then my car-mate Hussein shouted up to me to go and give him a hand with the car he was doing. I collected my rags and joined him. You do the tyres and dry them, he told me. I flashed him a happy smile from my mouth which hadn't seen a toothbrush for so long. The only way I brushed my teeth was with a finger after a meal or sometimes with a mairungi stick.

I hurried up with the tyres when he told me there were other customers of his waiting. This added to my joy. I felt like jumping for joy, for this would save me from hunger. And also the whole of the afternoon I would have been without mairungi. I felt that Hussein realised that my customers hadn't come today and this was just another favour he was doing me. I had done the same for him when his customers had failed to come and he was broke. This always happened to all the boys here. The car-washers.

It was around one when we finished and decided on lunch. We counted how much we had got from those three cars. We had fourteen shillings, and he gave me six. We went to Kwa Mama Kiosk. There we ordered double plates with two cups of Uji. From there we went for our afternoon killer, mairungi. After buying it we went back, passing through Sophia or Sophy. Under this sign I stopped and looked at the writings and the names on the wall of this church. The names read: Viet Nam, very shiny because the paint was still wet, followed by El Fatah, Black September, Ku Klux Klan, Black Panthers, Black Power, Fu Manchu, Black Sunday, Dracula, The Suicide Commando, CIA, FBI, Peace-Makers, Harlem, Black Ghettos, Cotton Comes to Harlem, Shaft,

6

IRA, Hare Krishna, Mau Mau, Anyanya, Mafia, Frelimo, Che Guevara, Castro, Dr Martin Luther King, Dr Nkrumah, Eduardo Mondlane, Malcolm X, Bangla Desh, Biafra, Mao, Karl Marx, Lenin, Amilcar Cabral, Kennedy, Sonny Liston, Clay, Lumumba, Hippies and many other names which I could not make out or whom they belonged to. I expect some belonged to organisations, political parties, freedom fighters, movies, politicians and boxers. It was Hussein who called me to get moving and we went back to Katanga Base to wait for business, while I was still wondering about the names and who the writer was.

We sat under the shade of the roof of this building which is a headquarters of Tanzania Club, as the sun was too hot for movement. The only disturbance was from this dust blowing now and then due to the wind. We waited, chewing our gatty. Those present were Burma, Rajab, Hussein, Jabbir, Odish, Yossa, Ally, Ahmed, Suleiman, Erick, Brazee, Amasco, Njirose, Yusuf, Kadugunye, Uha, Urai, Salim, Chinua, Juma, Bez, Mayanja, Gachui, Kachafu, Mkora, Omamo and Abbasi. Burma and Suleiman were the great talkers, and we liked them to entertain us at times like this when we had nothing to do. Burma could tell you any lie or any fact, whichever you preferred, and he was very good on the subject of politics. He believed in the two-party system.

He had a good memory and he could tell you the philosophy of Karl Marx or Lenin. He adored most the philosophy of Castro and Nyerere. He was a guy of six feet two, with a good frame of body for a south-paw boxer. He had a powerful voice. As for Suleiman, he was a liar. A liar with rotten teeth. A slim guy, once a musician in the Pan Africa Grill, Sombrero, Club 1900, and Swiss Grill. He was a great talker. He sometimes claimed to have gone to Mecca for hijra. A plain lie. He could turn a lie into a fact and it would remain a fact. He could tell you a lie so that it could take you a hell lot of time to argue with him. And to make it worse he knew quite well that it was a lie. The rest were all washers with little hope. So these two kept us busy with their lies while we in return nodded to put more steam into them. Then came this cheating singer Mwachi. A very funny nut. He was not a born musician but he was always forcing himself to that career. He too was a liar. He called me a name, trying to make people pay attention to him. No one bothered because he was known here as a great liar. I answered him back. I told him what kind of fool he was to be sharing a room with his in-laws. That cooled him. It was a fact about him. He hated me because of that.

So the topics went. They were now talking about the government and the opposition. How good the opposition was and how bad the government was, with the one-party system. I paid no attention. I only thought about the morning and those people I saw going into the church. How innocent were they? Were they really not sinners or was it true that they went there to pray for the dirty seeds they planted last night, some for them to succeed and some for them to fail? I think some went to pray to God to safeguard their riches. My thoughts went on next to that Benz man. Education is shit, I concluded. Then my mind came to rest on the writings on that wall. Was is it Bond, Sambo, Baker Massopo, PC, or Jabbir who wrote them? The boys of Sophia with no hope. And did those people of Din Roho let them write all those names there, and why? The sect which always locked its doors and windows when praying. This thought so troubled me that I decided to go and have a look again. I'm coming back, I told Hussein, in case my customers came. That was to enable him to come and call me. I'm going to Sophy.

Are you going to have some more?

No, I told him. He looked doubtful.

I crossed the road at this zebra crossing in front of the Mosque and headed back to the inscriptions again.

It was while I was looking at them, absorbed in thinking about these names, when this guy Massopo came from the back, staggering. He was drunk. He said, Hello brother, in a very hoarse voice.

Hello, I said back. He came and stood beside me.

How do you dig it, man? he asked.

Fine, man, I said. Looks good.

Yeah, man, I dig it meself, he said, applying the American slang. That was how he always was when drunk. Not only him, but all

8

the Sophy gang. They were one thing one time and another time the other.

You do? I asked, to mock him.

Yeah brother. I dig it good.

Sure, I said. But tell me, who do they all belong to? That was another mockery because Massopo was brainy, though he looked a failure in life because of too much daily drinking and the dope. Bhang.

Ah, that is simple man, he said, and began. Viet Nam is where there is a war between the Vietnamese and the Americans. The Americans wanna rule them but they don't wanna. I tell you death there is like drinking tea. People are dying like chickens. It happens any time. I think you heard about that Lt Cally?

Yeah, I said. The one who massacred a whole village.

That's the life there.

Then he went on: El Fatah, these are Arab guerrillas who hijack planes for ransom. They time-bomb, kidnap and kill. And so too are the Black September. Ku Klux Klan, that's an American organisation which is very tough down the US there. Always clad in black robes and masks. Even Nixon fears them. Black Panthers, these are our fellow blacks in US, and Black Power is their soul cry. *Fu Manchu, Black Sunday* and *Dracula*, these are Christopher Lee's movies.

I guess you know this guy? he asked.

I have heard of him, I said.

How do you find his acting? he asked.

Horrible, I said. Very scaring.

Yeah, man, I like his acting. Have you heard about him? I mean the party he had? he asked.

No, I said.

He scared his wife so badly that it led to their divorce, he explained.

Sure? I asked.

Like hell sure. His wife thought that it might turn out one day to be real, all those things he always did to women, he said.

Eh! I remarked.

And on he went. The Suicide Commandos are Japanese war

9

men. Very dangerous and always on dangerous missions. When they fail they commit suicide. Harlem and Black Ghettos, these are like slums here. Just like the Slums, Makaburini, Mathare Valley and those along the Nairobi river. In US they call them Harlem and Ghettos. *Cotton comes to Harlem* and *Shaft* are movies, and I tell you, man, the blacks soon gonna take over from the whites, he said.

Yeah, I supported him. I wish we beat them like how we are doing in boxing and athletics, I said.

IRA, this is the Irish army and I tell you man they are giving the British a hard time there in Ireland. Just like the Vietnamese to the Americans. They don't allow their women to be seduced by the British. If one is found she is shaved quite clean and then decorated with black tar. Hare Krishna, this is a new sect in town here with its followers shaved clean with only a small part left in the centre of the head. Almost like Yul Brynner and that singer from the ghettos, Isaac Hayes. Mau Mau, oh man these are our freedom fighters in the forest who gave Lord Delamere a time to remember.

What do you mean, Lord Delamere? I asked.

I mean the British man. The British man will live to remember them during the struggle for uhuru. Do you know who their leader was? he asked.

I pretended that I didn't know. No, I said.

What tribe are you? You must be shit if you don't know who the hell Dedan Kimathi was. The British hanged him.

Too bad, I said.

Yeah, too bad, if it weren't for him uniting us we would still have been licking the white man's arse, he said.

You mean the British? I asked.

Damn you, yes, I mean them. Then he continued: Anyanyas, these are Sudanese rebels fighting Numeiry's army in Sudan. They have been fighting for the past sixteen years. Mafia are corrupt gangsters. It is an Italian organisation which has spread all over the world. They can corrupt anyone from a minister to a peasant. Frelimo, this is an organisation of guerrillas giving the Portuguese a hell of hard time in Mozambique. The leader, the late Eduardo

10

Mondlane, got assassinated by the imperalists with a time bomb. I think his wife must have been connected with his death. She was an American, and you know how whites are.

Yeah, I don't trust them, I said.

Che Guevara and Castro, these were two best friends and great revolutionaries before Che was killed in another attempt to have a coup in Bolivia, South America. They caused the revolution in the island of Cuba with a small number of other revolutionaries. Not numbering a hundred. Castro now is the leader and he has made the island so powerful that it scares America. Dr Martin Luther King is a civil rights leader, down there in US. No, he is dead. Some loose nut of a guy gunned him down. Dr Nkrumah ... Oh ... yeah. He was a communist down there in Ghana. He got toppled by ... let me think ... yeah ... General Ankrah, and do you know what that nut did?

No, I said.

Shit man, I tell you.

What did he do? I asked.

He nearly brought Ghana tumbling down, he said.

How? I asked.

Money. He grabbed all the money to get rich quickly, he said.

Eh. Sure? I asked.

Like hell sure. Man, these black leaders. I tell you they are horrible, too corrupted. He made the people want Nkrumah back, he said. But the guy died in exile. Then he went on: Bangla Desh is where there is war now. The banyans are fighting each other over Sheikh Mujibur and the detained Ali Bhutto. They want Ali Bhutto. Biafra is in Nigeria where that black-bearded General Ojukwu is leading rebels into war with General Gowon's army. He is, I mean Ojukwu, the son of a millionaire. But you know, I hate war.

Why? I asked.

Imagine eating rats and anything because there is no food. Imagine the millions of innocent lives that get lost, he explained.

Well, that's true politics, I said.

Do you like politics?

No, I said.

11

Well, don't ever think of war. And he went on: Mao . . . is . . . a . . . that old man, a great leader in China. He is the world communist chairman followed by his wife the world communist woman. He saved the Chinese when they were about to be wiped from the surface of this earth, he explained.

Why is he great? I asked.

He is leading the world's greatest population. Over nine hundred million people, he replied.

I whistled at that. Last time it was seven hundred, I told him.

I tell you, man, the Chinese are the most productive people in the world. He once swam in cold freezing water to support a Chinese declaration, he said.

Well, he was a man of the people, I said.

Not only that, he is the proudest leader. He vowed that he would never leave China for America for anything and do you know what? At last Nixon went to China himself and it took him three days before he saw him. It was a history. He continued: Karl Marx and Lenin were world communist thinkers too. Amilcar Cabral is a leader of political freedom fighters in West Africa. Kennedy was a good leader in America who some numskull gunned down. Lee Oswald, I think, by name. His brother also got gunned by an El Fatah or a Black September fellow. I tell you, politics. To hell with it. Sonny Liston and Clay are sportsmen.

Heavyweight kings in boxing. Lumumba, yeah. He was a national hero in Congo. A true leader of the Congolese. He was killed in an organised plot and dumped into acid to lose all trace of him. From there followed the trouble in Congo over leadership. Moise Tshombe wanted to be leader and so did nearly every army man. That included Kasavubu. It resulted in war. Tshombe hired a Belgian army led by that General Schramme. They got wiped out by this hot-tempered General Mobutu. He burnt them up in the forest when he asked them politely to come out and they refused. Schramme was lucky, he was sent back to Belgium. Tshombe escaped and died in exile.

As for hippies, these are filthy-looking war-runaways from America. They are sons of millionaires who don't wanna go into

12

the army to be sent to Viet Nam. You can see them in town, dirty and very rough.

I saw some at Base when they came for the dope, bhang, I said.

Yeah, did you see how they look? he asked.

Quite silly, I said. Bushy beards, dirty jeans; and also their dames. Silly impersonating characters, I said.

Yeah, some are even staying down there at Race-Course, he added.

But how about those two you left out? I asked.

Which ones? he asked.

CIA and FBI? I pointed to them.

Ah? Yeah, those are American intelligences. Secret agents. Like the British Scotland Yard.

It was well timed because just as he was finishing his clarification Hussein came running and calling my name, saying I was wanted. I thanked Massopo and handed him some haba or sticks which he didn't want to take because he was drunk. Instead he begged for a cigarette but I had none to give him. That was because I don't smoke fags. I gave him twenty cents instead to go and buy some.

Hurrying back to Katanga Base, we came to a stop at the zebra crossing. We stared towards the mosque. Somebody had kicked the bucket. He had been brought here for prayers on his way to hell. The people were so many that the traffic had come to a standstill. He must be a rich man or else he couldn't have collected this mass of people. That was how the Muslims or waSwahili of this place were. If you're poor, too bad for you. Very few people at your funeral. Five, six was not a bad number. They came for the food. But this one must be rich. With his corpse were these old men in kanzus, with turbans and tarabushis. Many of them, singing prayers for this dead man. They all disappeared into the mosque. Taxi-drivers all stared with open mouths. Hussein too left to join them. I crossed the road to go and see my customers. I would have joined him, but the only time I enter the mosque is when there is Maulidi or during the celebrations of Idd. Otherwise no. Reaching Base, I found my customer. He was a former member of the banned opposition party. A very cool man. Always in a

13

striped suit with his hair parted in the centre, making a nice lane for lice if he had any. He had been in detention and only came out some few months back. He talked little, and didn't allow anyone to wash his car when I was not around. His was a black Benz. After parking it he would stand aside or take a stroll around the Slums and come back after I had finished. Sometimes I would ask him for the ignition key so that I could move the car from the wet mud to a dry place. This was only to fulfil my dream which never would come true. A dream to possess a Benz. But I will die without it. May God bless poor me. I liked him, though on the side of paying he was not good. Sometimes I would wash and polish and he would only pay me eight shillings, following it in his deep soft voice about his own condition. You know, he would say, I'm just unemployed like you and you see to run this car I have to budget on the money that I have. I have a family of six, four boys and two girls and all in school. I have to pay the house-rent bills, the water and light. So you see I have all these problems to look at. I always sympathised with him. He was always frank with me. He would tell me, look here, boy, you're lucky the way you are. If you were in the boots of these people you see running around with cars you would laugh your head off. They only tolerate it because a man has to bear the burdens. And too bad if you were married. But then there are those first-class people, I would answer. People without a care in this world.

When I reached him, he greeted me. Boy, how are you?

Fine, I said.

Shkamoo? he joked. The Muslim greeting.

Marhaba, I answered.

How you pushing on? he asked.

Not bad. Then I noticed that he had two more men with him.

Still chewing goat's cuds? he asked.

He used that phrase when referring to our mairungi, our drug.

Yeah, I said. What else can I do?

Then be careful, God might soon change you into a goat, he joked.

14

I would be happy, I said. No more troubles would come to me.

They all laughed. They had such rich, deep voices that mine sounded like that of a virgin. Voices of justification.

Let me introduce you to my friends. Here is Dubo Onditi Rachier. He is the director of Survey. I looked at him carefully. He had the features of a man who had perhaps taken part in the world war. He must have seen many aspects of the beautiful life. He was very tall, around six foot three or so. And this one is Alego Ragar Chiew. He is the Dean of the political faculty in the University. He is a professor. I eyed him. He was not all that tall. And he didn't look even like a professor. He was a small man. Anyhow, that is how these Nyanza people are. Very learned. And here, gentlemen, he told them, you meet Eddy Onyango Boy. Boy was a nickname that he always called me whenever he came here.

Are you a Luo? asked Alego.

Why? I asked him.

Onyango is a Luo name.

Well, I am.

He made a face as if wondering to himself, and saying:

You are shaming our tribe. So you are Onyango?

Chot Nyiri, I added. Or Chura.

Eh? Yeah, you look like it. A loving type. That was Onditi

They all laughed as if it was the funniest joke of their lives. That annoyed me. It sounded like mockery to me. Foolery. Perhaps inwardly they were thinking, what a lost Luo boy to be living in Majengo. He can't be a Luo. Perhaps a Swahili-Luo, a son of no father. A two-shilling boy.

Well, Boy, Simba Thuondi – as was his name – went on, there are three cars here. He pointed to three Benz cars parked. His, a black one, a light blue one and a white one. We want them in an hour's time because we are attending a party tonight. A Russian CD. So hurry up. By the way, where is your other friend?

He is around, I said.

Okay. We want them in that time. In the meantime we are taking

15

a walk around the area and perhaps we might pop in for a short-time job in those tarts' houses. Okay? He joked.

Yeah, I said.

Be careful not to allow anybody in them.

I won't, I assured them. And with that they strolled towards the War Memorial Hall. Perhaps they were heading towards Massand-ukuni in the Mashimoni. Those were our bars around here in the Slums.

I didn't know which car to start with. Three to one. Too much. My mate Hussein hadn't come back. I looked at the others. They all had 'Call me' faces. I didn't like that. They didn't call me to help with theirs. That's how it was. People here were partners. I looked towards the mosque. This monkey Hussein hadn't come yet. I then called Rajab and told him to go and call Hussein for me. He didn't show signs of liking that. I repeated it again. He was in doubt what to decide. Then he chose to go. Within a flash he was back. He is coming, he said. I doubted that information. We then called for water. Still no sign of this nut. I got vexed. He must be silly to take all that length of time. I decided to go myself. I told Rajab to start with the rugs and tyres. I went towards the mosque. I didn't mind my state. At the gate I removed my shoes. But too bad for me because I met with Ambari at the gate, and as I was always in opposition to this religion he started chasing me out. *Toka nje wewe!* he shouted. Get out! I stood my ground. He repeated the remark again. I just stood there. Then this drew the attention of the others. Another one called me Kaffir. They were annoyed with me. I didn't mind about them. I only wanted to trace Hussein. Then this cheating pretending Sheikh came to me with his bakora waving it at me. *Toka nje bana! he said. Wamtaka nani?* Get out, mister. Whom do you want?

Hussein, I said.

Which Hussein? he asked.

Tongolo Mbili, I said. His nickname.

Okay, wait outside for him, he said.

I picked up my shoes and went out. Then Hussein came and asked me what the hell it was all about. It is your old men. Tell

16

them I'm not interested in eating the man's food. Especially that Ambari.

Leave them alone. What is it? he asked.

Business. That man left three cars and I'm all alone. Rajab is doing the rugs and the tyres. We went and did the cars. Finished, we waited for the owners to come. Something bugged me. I didn't like the way they had looked at me. I thought about buying new socks. But how would I wear them? With these stinking worn-out shoes? That would be silly. Then we saw them coming. They looked a bit drunk. Especially Alego. He seemed to be talking a lot. We watched them approaching. Ready? asked Simba Thuondi.

Yep, I said.

Then through the corners of my eyes I noticed Alego and Dubo surveying the cars. I heard the professor telling his friend, yes, they have done them. The other one agreed. Then he added, check if all things are okay, I don't trust these slum boys. That was in his mother tongue. Man. I felt it. That is the badness of this place. We are always suspected. I told him in the same tongue that stealing is not our habit. That surprised him. Perhaps he thought I hadn't heard him. *Mos*, he apologised. Sorry.

Then in a boastful voice they asked, how much?

I didn't know whether to lie or not. Perhaps they had been told what to give. I hesitated before saying fifteen. I looked towards the other friend to see if he might have heard what I said. He hadn't.

What? they asked.

Fifteen.

They looked at each other. Then at their friend Simba. There was something fishy. They said nothing. Only produced their wallets and fished out a pound each. I then approached Simba Thuondi.

Well, did they pay you good? he asked.

Again I didn't know whether to lie or not. I said, fifteen each.

What? I told them it was a pound.

Well, that's what they paid us.

I will ask them.

17

No. Don't bother. It is I who said that because they are your friends.

Well, if it was you then I won't ask. Okay, take this, and he handed me fifteen shillings. That was a surprise to me. Fifteen bob? A man who always gives me eight, sometimes six? Strange.

Then his friends hooted. He said bye and drove away. I thought what a mess the professor would be in when he reached his wife. He was being betrayed by his feelings. He must have popped in for a lay. A two-shilling lay with the wazibas or bamzis.

I shared the outcome of our sweat. I gave Hussein fifteen and Rajab ten. That left me with thirty.

It was now getting late. All the boys were storing their washing rags, and in doing so making sure that the sleeping places were okay. That there were no leakages in the wrecks. Ours was okay. We had strong new cardboard on the windows and good sacks. After the inspection we decided to go for our supper. The supper was just like our lunch. Ngunya. Adding on top of it our cheapest illegal brew, Changaa or Waragi or Cham or Machwara, Ching or Vyang or Machozi ya Simba, or Vitu or Wine or Pelele. The slum names for this brew. Gulping it down was called *Kutupa kwa Roho*. Apart from Ngunya we could have a change by taking Mbaazi na Mkate with the ten-cent coffee, a half glass. When you couldn't afford the brew you could go to dope. Bhang. Too much of it in the slums here. Called Safi, Weedy, Mashada, Njem, Makshabu, Njaga, Bangi, Tumbaku and Vitu too. Also Gabba.

We went to Rash's kiosk. We took Mbaazi na Mkate plus a full glass of ten cents coffee. We met Nyanjau, Sophia, Hadijah, Kangwele and Mary. Those of the slum girls with no hope of getting married. Mothers of two, three or four bastards. Sons of different fathers. Mother girls who can walk till morning with no one to rape them. All the slummers were bored and fed up with them. Nearly all the boys had laid them. Too cheap.

From there we went to Charia's place. The name of the place was 'Rest House Club 69'. The illegal brew was sold there. Hussein was with us but he didn't take the stuff. His stuffs were Gabba, petrol and Gatty. But we were thinking of giving up the latter, Gatty. We had found out that we lost appetite after chewing it. As

18

for petrol, he would soak a piece of cloth in a petrol tank and retire with it to our wreck of a car. He would inhale it till he fell asleep. That was after puffing the dope. He always made me wonder. I thought the next place for him would be Mathare Mental Hospital. As for me, it was only the dope and drink. Any drink that would get me drunk. This was because without it sleeping in the wrecks would be impossible. With all that cold of the night. As for wazibas, most of the boys found it hard to give out the hard-earned money to these two-shilling tarts. Only sometimes when drunk. And that too would be a helluva lot of time before a mziba would allow you in. They didn't like drunks. To give out our two shillings to these tarts was a problem. It was only due to the satisfaction of human nature that sometimes we were forced to do it. And that again depended. You might go and buy the thing, perhaps when a guy with VD had been to it. That would be too bad if you were married and perhaps only trying to steal. You would all pay a visit to the STC. Dr Mustafa would be very glad to see you. That doc has seen so many people that I thought in his dreams he must be dreaming about them. I remembered when once I got into friendship with it. Man, it was terrible. It was when I was a local musician. The silly infectious job for the VD if you were a playboy. It was at Athi River where we had gone to perform for the Jamhuri celebration. It was this guy Phillip who fooled me into it. He seduced a tart and told me to go and have fun with him. That was how I got it. It took me two weeks to find out what was wrong with me. By then I was in school. No money for private docs and I was afraid to tell. Man, it was shit. Shit. I was forced to go to STC. that dispensary. It is on your right from Shauri Moyo, the slum city of leaning trees. Near the bridge on your left and on your right from Shauri Moyo. If you pass there watch the men and see how the sun is torturing them in the line hiding their faces to the wall. See the gloomy faces hidden with newspapers. This clinic. Whoever thought of building it there knew where to punish men. I was one of them. Inside Mustafa demanded to see me. I got the injection from this fat woman who mocked me saying that I was studying books in the daytime and women at night. Why didn't you come to me? she asked me. Or is it because I look old? She made me feel guilty. I haven't gone back since. It left me crowned with small pimples.

At Charia's the stuff was not enough. We took half a glass each. Charia complained that the flatfeet, meaning cops, were around. And that he had not enough cash to corrupt them with. We had nothing else to do. We thought of Mama Atieno's place. Njoroge, being thirsty, proposed Italo's place. A car-washer too. That was Rajab. It brewed up an argument between the boys. No, Burma supported him. Italo's stuff is not okay. They added water to it, diluting it.

That stuff doesn't come from Kisumu like that of Atieno, said I. I think it is the one from Mathare.

Yeah, agreed Burma. And have you seen what that is made from?

No, said Rajab.

You would hate changaa. You would hate drinking it.

OK then. To Mama Atieno's.

We left for the place.

We took the way behind the hall, the path between Sophia Hotel and the Pumwani African Bar. The path was dark, only supplied with a dim light from this public toilet. It was full of human shit which was left by both young and old, men and women. Very beautifully arranged in a row along the bamboo cane as a fence around the bar. The path was very private because at a time like this people didn't pass here. We took it. Then reaching this stunted bush of a flower we came to a stop. It was me who heard the noise. It was so faint that you could mistake it with those made by the movement of cats. Cats are so many here at this time. At last I heard the voice. It was the female. I knew why. So on hearing the voice I indicated to the others to stop. I listened again. No sound came. I wasn't sure. I heard a sound, but of a human not a cat.

Then I asked for a match box. Asked Burma, what for?

Just for something, I said.

Here Brazze gave me. I picked a paper and felt it heavy. It had some smell; I dropped it. Shit. I looked around for another one.

What is it? asked Hussein.

Wait and see, I said.

Come on, what is it? That was Njoroge. They were all anxious. I picked a paper and this time I was more careful not to pick a shitted one. I lighted it and approached the stunted flower. I lifted it up. Bent to peep underneath. The light reached them. A man and a woman.

We all bent down to look at them. And we knew who they were when we saw them. Shit, we cursed. We left them.

The slob and his woman. We had even forgotten about Cham. We hurried to Mama Atieno's place. There we found Captain Drunkards and his friend Dad Madebe. With some unknown faces too. We ordered two guns. Two full bottles of Teacher's Whisky. Like a flash, because it was an illegal drink and the Government was very harsh about it, we gulped it down. Also because Atieno tipped us that the cops, the corrupted cops were around. We paid a pound and left with everybody agreeing on the stuff. It got us fast. We ran amok. We started the unnecessary noises. The wise noises of the drunks. Everyone talking out his silly logic while on the way hooking and elbowing whoever we meet with. Then ahead of us between these Transfer Traffic trailers we saw people, a group sitting. Some, four or five standing. We knew who they were. The cops. But it was too late. Some six or seven had surrounded us. All with batons. We just didn't know how they did it. I think they heard us shouting and so hid between these trailers. Or perhaps at Ukumbusho. *Simama yote,* they commanded us. Stop.

Kitu gani? asked Brazze. What is it?

Walevi? Drunkards? they roared.

Who is a *mlevi?* asked drunk Njoroge. Rajab couldn't say anything. The stuff was too much for him. I, in turn said nothing. I didn't like being rude to the cops. Especially these of the Slums. They can frame anything on you. Or beat the hell out of you down there in the police station. These of ours are brutes. Nothing but real living brutes.

Do you want to be thick-headed? asked one with the accent of a Kalenjin.

No, we all said when we noticed one of them approaching with a dog. Man, that killed my heart. The sight of the dog. I don't like

21

the play of this animal. He came and stood at a distance. We said nothing more. We joined the sitting group. More were rounded up. They joined us. Then, having got enough of us, they decided to march us to Shauri Moyo. Two by two, they ordered. We joined hands. But? They started calling us aside one by one. Ah. It is the daily game here. The usual game. The bribe. We came to this toilet and we were bundled into it. Those who had something to offer. We gave them what we had. Brazze gave three shillings. I gave out ten for three of us. Me, Hussein and Burma. The others too gave what they had. Njoroge had only a shilling. That went. These people must be gaining easy money. But who wants to go to Makadara Court and be fined forty shillings? Five is okay. What is left you booze up in the new day. We left the have-nots behind.

On our way we complained about the corrupted cops. What do you say, boys? asked Burma. What do you say?

What else but corruption, said I.

May God bless Africa, said Brazze. Were it not for that brute of a dog they wouldn't have got me, Brazze continued.

I'm never friendly with dogs, I said. They are like deaf dumb mutes, when you are crying painfully they think you are happy laughing. They won't stop until they see blood.

Well, they are the law, said Burma.

Then, talking less, we retired to our wrecks. Our happiness was gone. In the car no wink of sleep came. I started thinking. I was sober.

If anybody had told me that one day I would come to live in this place and, worse, in these wrecks, I would have knifed him. Nobody wanted to be told such a thing. No one wanted to be called Mtu wa Majengo. Majengo or Pumwani was and is still considered to be the most evil corrupted place in the whole of Nairobi. And that is true. Tell anybody that he is from this place and see what will follow. The Slums as it was to me was evil. And corrupted. In the old time if it was heard that you had been to Majengo you were automatically an outcast. If you had a new bride that night you couldn't share a bed with her. The next day she would be gone. Every one feared the place. A city of two shillings malaya. A place

22

of waSwahili. A place where most of the children are sons and daughters of malaya. If a father was told that his son had been to Majengo that day he would sleep out. He would be cursed with all the dogs and cats of Lucifer. All the gods and satans. A father might kill his son even. Whoever went there was considered to have gone for the two-shilling fun. That was the first thought, followed by spirit. Spirit. This was the commonest drink of the place. It was being sold at Digo. And that is how the name Digo still exists. It was a name that most of the senior Nairobi dwellers knew. The old men who were lifetime drinkers. But one thing they never thought of. That some of the leaders or ministers could come from this place. And it is very strange that when they were passing through here they wound up all the car windows. They didn't want the smell of dust. They were even proposing that the Slums be demolished, forgetting that they too once dwelt here. That it was a disgrace to the whole city, forgetting that it was the mother city of Nairobi. It was only a mile or so from the city centre. The houses were built of mud. The roofs of tin. Very brown rusted tin. With alleys or paths between the mud houses full of shit. Left by all the young and old men and women.

I came to Majengo when things fell apart. That was when he got retired from work. I mean my old man. He got retired due to old age. And in fact he was old and worn out. If an old man went to both world wars at the age of fourteen he is old by now. From world wars he joined the railways, having been to Portugal, Burma and some other places that he couldn't recall because of illiteracy. He was too young to lift or carry a gun, so he was always carrying luggage. One time he nearly got nailed. The bullets riddled the luggage on his back and one cut him on the knee, leaving the cut for him to remember the war by and as a proof for his children to see whenever he told the story of war. He used to pull up his trousers and show the mark, swearing that no son of his would ever join the army or any other force. That is while he was alive. But how wrong he was. He never knew that things would one day change so that even getting that job of carrying luggage in the army would be hard to find. That finding any job nowadays was a problem. I wished he had lived long enough to see. To see how the

23

city is nowadays. How good and lucky it was to find a job. Even that of RV with your Cambridge certificate in the City Council. Unless your kin was one of them, Directors or Managers or that, and unless you gave out four masais. Four hundred shillings. And sometimes even then you might fail to secure one. And I guess you know what would follow. A hungry dog fighting against a well-fed boss. The law would judge.

So from the war he joined the railways. By then people were forced to work. They were chased from anywhere when it was heard that a fellow with no job was fooling around. You couldn't look for a job two days without finding one. Standard eight was the topmost in the fifties. And now they are the bosses giving the form fours and the graduates a hell of a time. They are afraid that nowadays the school leavers might topple them from their chairs in the offices.

With the railways he was given a house at Makongeni Miksi. The place where we were all born. A family of ten. Unlucky for my two brothers who died in infancy. We remained eight. Three ladies and five gentlemen. The ladies were Dommy, Tandra, and Atiesh. The boys were, Ocholla the eldest, then Wanga Muriu. Muriu was a nickname because his best friends were Kamau and Njoroge and Kiama. They were all crooks. They operated their hooliganisms in Bahati and Majengo. At that time there were no Ofafa Jericho, Jerusalem, Uhuru, no new flats of Kariokor, Pumwani, Otiende, Moi, Ngei, Madaraka, Jamhuri or these estates. Only three were very important, and those were Bahati, Makongeni and the old Kariokor. And also Pangani.

After Wanga came Oyoyo, Benny, and Eddy, that's me. I'm the bottomest among the boys, followed by Atiesh and then Tandra. So in Okongo, as the place is sometimes called, we were born. In that Miksi of 0. 8. And that is where I saw the starting of Mau Mau. And how we used to get awakened in the night when the johnnies were conducting the search for Mau Maus. With their guns and bonnets. After waking everyone, we were all led to the football field and made to sit on our heels. Crouch. By then I was young but wise. No unemployed were wanted in the city. No visitors were wanted in Makongeni, unless they were railway workers. For a

Kikuyu to come into town he had to have a Pass. In that Pass was indicated the place he was going to, and to whom, and the time. If he failed to leave in the time shown a search was conducted for him. The home-guards did it. If he was found then it was too bad for him. Those home-guards are now the bosses.

So in Makongeni we lived till my dad fell sick. It was due to Sepe, as we call them in the Luo tongue: old spirits. Some sharp tongues said he was mad. Those midomo mirefus. I tell you, some humans. That forced his retirement. And it was after he had been taken to Mathare Mental Hospital. It was all a waste, because Sepe cannot be cured with any white man's medicine. It is only controlled by Buru kod Manyasi, some ashes and herbs. With a goat's skin, Pien diel and Mtembes. And Gagi. All black man's magic.

From Makongeni, after the declaration of the Emergency, when things cooled down, we left for Kisumu. That was to take dad for the cure of his Sepe or Juogi.

From Kisumu he came back and looked for a job. He got one with the City Council. Cutting grass around the locations. And that was to get us educated. Ocholla and Wanga were not all that bad. They had learned to standard eight and six. Wanga was too much of a crook and so standard six was as far as he could go. His crookedness landed him in Kabete Approved School, a place where many of the Nairobi crooks once lived. Some even now. But juveniles. That was when he got arrested for some picking at Bahati with his friends. They had with them a gun.

With the council job a house was supplied at Ofafa Kunguni or Ofaro, where by then many houses had no residents. So many were vacant that we used to shit in them. I wonder how it is that the population has grown so quickly that to find a house today is worse than finding a job. At that time only one large building existed. That was Friends' Centre. I like that place because it is where I learnt the 'On my Honour', the Scouting. That was free because we had aided in planting the grass around. Mr Walter was in charge. Followed by Njenga. And then there was one old man who was a night-school teacher. He was Daudi. I wonder if he is still living. It is so many years back. Recently I popped over there and got chased away because I'm not known. Funny.

So dad cut grass while we struggled hard for education. Benny and Oyoyo at St Michael, while I was now at the old church, the old building of Our Lady of Visitation. Atiesh and Tandra were at St Anne's. In 1959 he left the City Council and joined a motor firm. The job was again another silly one. Sweeping three of the four blocks of a camp. That was at Mbotela. An even sillier job, especially where children don't go to school and have stubborn mothers. He was always quarrelling with them. At last he played deaf, just for the sake of it. Then came the idea of retiring old people. He got retired with his small pension. By then we were half way through the secondary, the boys, not the girls. That started the trouble of looking for a house in Nairobi. We found one, but it was too expensive: in Eastleigh. The rent was Shs. 200 a month. A single-bedroomed house. That was too much for our family. Then Dommy, who by then was already married, thought of an idea. There was a relative of her former husband at the offices of the City Council at Eastlands. He was in charge of the housing department. She went there and asked for this Silla. She found out that that slob had been sacked some time back. This nut wanted to marry her in the first instance. Then she asked for Aricka. She found him and told him the family trouble. That nut also worked with dad during his time with the City Council. The man did his best and we got a house at Gorofani. But we didn't enjoy the life of that house. It was a short-lived one. Dad and mama were on their way to Kisumu when the bus OTC had an accident at Kericho. They all died. On receiving the news we all left for home for the burial ceremony. We were away three months. When we came back a new Mkamba face was in our house. When we asked him how, the reply was, go and ask the City Council. At Eastlands the answer was simple. Rent. Three months' rent.

And that was the starting of a new life. Things fell apart. We split up. Each to manage on his own. Tandra and Atiesh went to Dommy's. Ocholla down to Kijiji, Mathare Valley slums, where I understand he is now the first brewer of Changaa. Wanga, nobody knows. Benny had some luck. He joined the Air Force.

Breaking dad's vow that no son of his would join the forces, if he was still alive. He feared the hard tough life of a soldier during a war. You would drink your own urine sometimes when there was no water in the forest. Or drink the mixture of water and blood in a river. As for the police, you might have to arrest even your mother, because it was the law. The police were in charge of cutting down a self-hanged fellow from a tree. That is a taboo to a Luo. As for the prison service, you might be handcuffed to a murderer, a man on his way to the grave. But what could anyone do on such an occasion, when he wanted to live? So he joined. As for Oyoyo, he is selling water in the slums of Kibera. And helping in selling busaa in the evenings in that Kilombero bar. Me, I joined the Slums. Sleeping in the wrecked old cars and washing cars. And I heard that Atiesh eloped with some chap. Well, that is not bad. Let her try her luck in that. Men don't want to marry nowadays. They are more keen on drinking. Too bad for the ladies. Too bad for sugar-mamas in town. Nowadays they are paying their dowries to young men to live with them. I wish I had got one. The other one working while I sleep all day waiting for the night work. Isn't that a crazy good idea, man? You sleep all day, wait for the night. In return you get anything. A car, perhaps, if she has one. Quids. Clothes and money. An idea.

It was here in Katanga Base that I joined the rest of the boys. As for the name, Katanga, I hope you know very well about that famous copper region in Congo. The region that Tshombe claimed as his. With all the copper. Some leaders are crazy. These blacks. And Base? Don't worry. That's a problem for you to work out. Katanga Base was easy to find. Right here in the Slums. It was opposite the War Memorial Hall, the chief's camp and the mosque. It was also a stage for taxis. And a garage too. Any model of car could be found here. The homes of the boys. Car-washers. All knowing how to drive. Good footballers. In fact, good at anything. Games and politics.

It was late night when sleep came. By then Hussein had turned four times, snoring and gassing out his carbon.

2

Monday morning, I was wide awake. We remained in the car. In the morning business didn't come. Hussein went out and bought the twenty-cent gabba. We puffed it. Nearly everybody was puffing. In the cars. Burma got out, urinated on their Zephyr and went back. Then after some time they all got out. I remained and checked the hideout of my GCE certificate. It was getting worn out. Because of the times I had carried it around trying for a job. I felt like tearing it up. It had no use. Some years back but not now.

Some years back you needn't walk a day with it. But now it is shit. And I mean real shit. Human shit. I think I will soon wipe myself with it. A paper is only good for that purpose. I'm not a Muslim to carry a tin with me to the toilet, with water. I looked at it and the every day's memories came. The sacrifice my dad made to have his sons educated and the outcome now. The good things he never did with his money, drinking and whoring about like these men I see daily around here looking for these wazibas at the end of each month and with their mid-month pay. What he couldn't have done with that small pay of fourteen shillings in the railways, at a time that when you were found with a pound note by the white man you had to tell how you came to have it.

Then the eighty-five shillings in the City Council and the two hundred and fifteen with the motor firm. He never drank or smoked. He knew no fashions. Only khaki shorts, kinyasa and a khaki shirt. On his foot the Akalla shoes. I think I won't marry. What is a wife for? What is a wife and children for in this world of mine? I wouldn't send them to school. Why? Afterwards to wash cars like me?

Never! I will never marry. When you are single, not many

28

problems. When you marry you work twice as much to feed the glutton wife. And when she gives birth as a result of your daily loving, you work three times as much. No, I won't marry any Eve, Lucifer or Delilah. I think that man of a god made a mistake in that. Torturing Adam to create a woman who brought nothing of profit but only poverty. A gate of death for the rich and the poor.

May a dog crush whoever thinks of marriage between me and her. It brings nothing but miseries. After looking at it I stuck the certificate back into its hideout. I then joined the boys, who were looking at the newspaper. We went through this *Nation* paper. Nothing very interesting. The headline and a good splash was about the raided shop last night. Cheating newspapers, I thought.

It was nearing noon, after lazing about the whole morning in the sun, when we thought of lunch. I was brooding. It was Hussein who got me out of it.

What are you thinking? he asked.

Nothing important, I said.

Or is it the money the police took from you?

No, I said

What is it then? he asked.

Nothing important, I replied.

So you won't tell me? he asked.

Well, if you are dumb, deaf and mute, keep on asking me, I replied.

Okay, keep it to your chest and tell it to the dogs, he remarked.

Yes, and you can lick your arse, I said.

He didn't know that today I needed no disturbance.

Let's go to Kwa Mama. I have only two shillings, he said.

We left.

In the afternoon, with ngunya in our stomachs, feeling lazy, we chewed the drug, miraa, waiting for business. The sun too hot for any movements. I went for water in the Safi kiosk. Safi was dozing his head off. I thought it was because of too much doping, the gabba, but he was wise. His head was on the cash-box. From there

29

I didn't feel like sitting in that heat. I headed straight for the hall.

I crossed the road and went to the hall. In the main hall badminton was in progress. Challenging the boys were these two ladies, Rash and Deborah. Others including Hadijah, Mamu, Waïthera, Wangare, Fatuma, Amina sat around. On the stage, table-tennis went on. Stunted figure of Saides Kibarango vis Maendeleo. Others waited. I got bored. I entered the billiards and snooker room. On the table were J.B., Set, Osman, Lucas, Abdy, Sir Ben, and Dika. They were playing Russian Pool as they called it. It was a gambling game where you had to pot one red and check your number of the colour if it is either blue, yellow, green, pink, black or brown. If it is one of them pot it. You take the money. Any amount that you are betting. Around seated on the benches were some players waiting to join and some spectators. Mostly the jobless. Waiting to join were Dudus, Lord Zangaro, Waimeri, Dalla, Mungai, Patty, Abbich and Gabbir.

So I squeezed in a corner and watched the game. Most of the luck fell on J.B., Abdy, Sir Ben and Osman. Then Lucas and Dika resigned. In joined Dudus and Lord Zangaro. The game went on. And so did the bet. When it reached one pound Sir Ben and Dudus resigned. Dalla and Waimeri joined in. Abdy won. Pound, pound, they echoed. Abdy won. Then it reduced to ten, ten. Abdy betted and said that he was going for a piss. He was wise. He didn't come back. They complained. But to whom? He was gone. They played. I got bored. Time for business was drawing close. I left and went back to Katanga Base. I found the boys busy. Those whose customers had come. I needed a puff and so I looked for Rori. He was a dealer. A peddler. He was not around. I asked Safi, a peddler too, in that tea-kiosk. No stock. Shit. I felt like I would go crazy without it. He told me that the stock from Kampala and Kisumu hadn't come. That he had been to Ziwani to that supplier and found none. Musumar too had none. Shit. Beautiful Moses. What was wrong today? I felt bad. No, I couldn't help it. I crossed the road. The Sophy. Suleiman must be having some. On my way I started thinking of how I got into the world of puffing the bhang. I thought of how we used to buy them at Uhuru market on the railway line to Nanyuki opposite Makongeni. They were sold like njugu, groundnut. Wrapped nicely in this toilet paper. And arranged beautifully on a tray or box. You couldn't see the owner, the peddler. He was among the crowd. What you did was only to place or drop a ten-cent piece on the tray and pick one roll. I used to watch my friends smoke. I would puff once, then twice, then thrice. That way I got into the world. The world of dope, cannabis sativa, bhang, gabba, mashada and more.

At Sophy, I found Suleiman with the last roll. I took it. I puffed around the hall. But god. What poor stuff! All makshabu. The whole of it is makshabu. Silly cheating fool. He had stolen my twenty cents for raprap. Monkey. Well, that cooled me. But poorly. I wondered how I could get out of this puffing world. I didn't know what I would have done without that one. I went back to Katanga Base.

On reaching I found this bearded guy with glasses waiting for me. With his white Ford Lancia. This guy was a nut. He made his father commit suicide. The old man hanged himself. He lived down there opposite Labour Ward. He was the only son and during his schooling time his father sacrificed himself till he got a scholarship to go and study in London. He went to study economics. Once there he paid no attention to his studies. He got into life. Blew ten years there and got married to one of the white baboons. So the nut got married and came back. He got a job with City Council as a piper. He didn't inform his parents that he was coming back. But the word got to them. One morning the old mzee with a black kuku, in his kabuti and Akalla shoes with his odunga, his walking stick, asked around and came to know the place of his living. When the old man knocked on the door, the white woman peeped through the spy-hole.

And that was because the old man was an intruder. Instead of pressing the knob of the bell he used his odunga. The woman got scared at the black gorilla she saw at her door. Then she opened. What do you want? she asked.

The old bagger knew no English. He thought he was being greeted.

Jambo mama, he said.

31

Mizuri, fine, she said. Perhaps that word she got taught when being loved. The time when all men are silly.

Nyumba ya Onyango? House of Onyango? asked the old man.

Onyango? asked the woman.

Ndiyo. Yes, answered the old man.

Then the old man saw the picture of his son hanging on the wall. He pointed to it.

The woman looked at it.

Mimi baba yake, he said. I am his father.

She looked at it and saw some resemblance to the old man.

Yes, she said. Then her son came and stood at her back. He was called Charles. That creole. He took one sight of the old man and gave out a yelp. That was because the toothless baboon tried to smile at him. He saw the red gums. The yell was too much. The woman got annoyed. She banged the door in the face of the old man. The old man sat on the grass. The woman rang her husband and explained everything. And with most stress on Charles crying. It took him little time to come home. And five minutes to get out of the car. He approached his old man. *Ang'o midwaro?* he asked. What do you want?

The old man stood damn dumb.

Ng'ano ma onyisi ka? Who directed you here? asked the son.

Apenjo. I asked, answered the old man.

Wach gima okeli. Tell me what has brought you, commanded the son.

The old man understood that he was not welcome. He told him that his mother was sick and perhaps by now she might even be dead.

So what if she is dead? She is old. Why did you leave her alone? asked the son.

I came to tell you so that you may come and see her for the last time, said the old man.

I can't stop her from dying, he roared at the old man. And all the time his wife peeping from behind, hiding Charlie behind her buttocks.

Here, take this, he said, and handed the old man a hundred-shilling note. The old man took it and begged for water. The husband went in and told his wife to give the old man water. The water was brought in a glass. When the old man drank it and handed back the glass, the glass fell and got broken. The husband came out holding one of his suits. He handed it to the old man. The mzee refused. He handed back the hundred-shilling note. He bent, picked up his bag and shed tears. Bitter tears. He cursed education and the white man. The mother had died when the old man reached home. He took the noose. So this Onyango was known around here. Just because of that sad story about him.

Hullo, I greeted him.

Hullo. Where were you? he asked.

Just around, I said.

I have been waiting for you, he said.

Don't worry. So as usual? I asked.

Yeah. As usual, he said.

I collected the rags and did the car. Hussein too was doing another car. Everyone busy. In the late evening we finished. We counted the outcome. Not bad. We went for supper. We had enough so that eating 'ngunya' was not welcome tonight. We left for Sophia Hotel. There we took karanga na chapati. At least we needed a good change. For tomorrow who knows what might happen? From Sophia Hotel we took to Mama Atieno's. It is the fruit of our Uhuru. That is waragi. From there we lost each other. I was so drunk that I didn't know how I dragged myself to the car. And I must have been very lucky because Geekay was not around. He picks pockets.

In the morning I realised that Hussein hadn't slept in the car. Then he came and told me where he had slept. He had slept at Fatuma's. The old pimp. That Fatuma Mwana. I hate her. She is very old compared to the others who are always at her place. She likes young men. She is over thirty and barren. Married once and got the sack. Because of knowing too much and the silly moves. The two-timing. It is the way of most of these women here. These waSwahilis. In her house are for sale Ritah, Flo, Muna Horse, Maia and Florence. Of all Fatuma is the oldest. Ritah too once married and got the sack. She is a sister of both Flo and Maia, who are still students. Florence is a drop-out student. The daughter of

33

a minister. How she came to be living in Fatuma's nobody knows. In that mud house with green painted windows. In there beer is sold. So when you got drunk there was no problem. You pay a pound to Fatuma and pick your choice. That is how Fatuma earns her living. Through others.

After he had told me the story I told him that I was taking a walk down to Industrial Area. He wished me luck.

On my way to Industrial I met with my friend Konga. He lived in that city, the city of leaning trees, Shauri Moyo. We met on this small bridge joining Kamukunji and Gorofani. He told me that he was going to work, and that he had left the ESA Bookshop and joined the Wanyee Books. After that, with his sympathies about my unemployment, he gave me a roll which he had hidden in his socks: We parted. I crossed and took the way up towards the stadium. Passing these trees I remembered the reason Konga once gave me. That was when we were puffing. He told me that these trees are that way because whoever planted them was a silly nut. He was a jealous fellow. He kept them so far apart that it was hard for them to copulate. The reason for leaning is that they are trying to kiss. I passed this kiosk with Kiroko at it selling the dope. I said hello and moved past. He had resigned from going to Labour. He had had six years without a job. I passed these other kiosks plus the timber yard. And the blacksmiths hammering out. I crossed the Jogoo Road, formerly Donholm, at the roundabout. I took the path behind the Shell BP. At the railway I checked the railway police. These guys hid in these shambas in plainclothes. They had arrested me three times for that kanyaga business. Trespassing. At the gates of EAI I joined the kibarua casual job hunters. We waited at the gate. We stood till we got tired and sat on the grass. No mention of vibaruas. I crossed this Commercial Street and joined the ones at UNGA Ltd. No luck came. I moved ahead. Towards the Labour Exchange. On my way I passed this Mangal son. This Singh must be rich. He always passed us down there at the Slums in different cars. I crossed on my right, passing the wine firm. Behind the wheels of a kombi sat this slummer, Pocomoco. He recently got a job with them. I waved at him and moved on. Passing

34

these firms and the newly built MOW Training School. At Labour I entered the clerical section. Damn place. The unemployed.

This timber-tinned building ought to be demolished, I thought. There is no warmth here. I squeezed into a corner. I looked at the blackboard. Quite innocent. No writing on it. All the people wearing sad faces. These guys must be suffering. They have no happiness. So mean with their fags. You would think that they didn't smoke. No one wanted to share his fag. Then came this Legion Maria fellow with rosaries dancing on his chest. With him a long tall crucifix. A black pope, I thought. He must be familiar because everyone is greeting him. Then this guy knelt in front of this black pope. They prayed. The place was quiet. Finished, the murmuring started. Then this pope was offered a place on a bench. Questions were fired at him. Where will Jesus come to when he comes back to earth? one asked.

When Jesus comes he will stand on the Got Ramogi in Kisumu. That is where all the people will see him. It is where the judgement will be delivered, he answered.

And where is your church? asked another.

At Makongeni. You can come there every evening for prayers.

Is it true that people fall down and talk without their knowledge, with saliva oozing out from their mouths? asked another.

Yes, that happens when the satans are running away from their souls.

And why don't Muslims eat pork? asked another. Everybody shut up to listen to the answer to that question.

That is a very good question, my friend, said the man. I will tell you why. The reason why the Muslims don't eat pork is that when their prophet Mohammed died it took them three days before burying him. When they came for him they found half of his bottom already eaten. And beside him sleeping peacefully was a pig. That caused it. The laughter. I wondered what would have happened if Ambari had heard this nut.

Then this door was opened and in came this guy looking beautiful and smart in his well starched khaki uniform. On his shoulders shone the medals of NYS and on his head the green beret. On it another medal of a crown. Down below shone the black boots. But his face was not all that beautiful. He had protruding teeth. You would think that he was laughing. Every one paid attention. All those who haven't registered their names should follow me, with their certificates. Also their IDs. We rose and followed him, something that I have done for the past years. And with no success. In the other room behind this same table with the worn-out name on it sat Ndege. He registered the names and told us to go and wait in the same room where we had been before. Those new to the procedure thought that the job was in hand.

We went back. The Legion Maria man still entertained the jobless. They had forgotten their troubles for some time. Then I formed a friendship with this Coast guy, Hamisi. A jobless too. We talked, getting acquainted with each other. Then joined another. He was Ngugi. We told him that he looked like one famous writer in US. He said no, but that guy was his cousin. So we talked of our troubles. Then we decided to take a tour at the back. Man, we wondered what hope have these people. They were tired of looking for jobs. They were playing cards, draughts and ajua or bao. Most of them were old men. I think they were the only happy people here. They didn't mind a damn. They had perhaps worked so many times before that now to work or not was the same to them. We moved in with them. On our right the food kiosk still stood. This woman should be a millionaire by now, she had collected so many coins of the jobless. She sold irio, vegetable and maize diet. And to wash it down was uji porridge. On our left the other kiosk. This one sold tea, toast and fags. Still hanging on the roof of the yard were the loudspeakers. They were for announcing the jobs and the required particulars. On the wall the innocent blackboard smiled. The clean-swept cement platforms were all occupied. I felt like drinking water. I excused myself. I went to the tap beside the blackboard. I gulped it down. I felt like pissing. I went to the toilet. I filed in behind those I found in there. The smell. More beautiful than any cosmetic smell. Too sharp for the nose. The paint was now brown. Because of the art done on it with shit. Some guys can do art. No need of going to universities. Or perhaps they were done by graduates, those on the tarmac.

I got into one. Terrible. The door all had the new paint. Shits.

To push the door you had to use your foot or clench a fist. Or elbow it or push it with your buttocks. You could butt it. And that was if you were a judoist. That was not all. The shits were piling on top of each other. The pump was out of date. On them were the maize cobs. Some packets of fags. I pissed looking up, trying to reach my nose to the window to have some fresh air. I started reading the writings on the walls. One made me smile. It was *Nitapata kaze wapi?*: Where will I get employment? That was it. I didn't take long. The stink could kill. It was good only for flowers. Out, I joined Hamisi and Ngugi. We moved, wondering about the employment. Then we came back to our section. Then this fellow came, Mutungi. He was my schoolmate. He failed the Cambridge. But since his dad is Minister of Labour he took no time. He got one as a Wages Inspector. A job that needed higher education. Hello, I said.

Ah. Hello, he said back. How are you, man?

Not bad. Just still on the tarmac, I said.

That is too bad, he said.

Yeah. But what can we do? I asked.

Nothing, man, nothing, he said.

So what are you nowadays? I asked. You look smart in your uniform.

Well I did an exam but flunked. It was for senior promotion, he answered.

Ah. That was bad, I said.

Not very, really. I'm soon doing another. But this time I will do what I can, he said.

Try, man. You might get promoted and fix us, I said.

But that is not very easy, you know. It needs a lot of influence, he said.

You will have the influence once you are there, said I.

Well, we will see, he said. It depends.

Now where are you going to, because you look on your way to some place? I said.

I'm going to some firms to have some checking down the Industrial, he answered.

Well, not bad. With us, we are still here. Trying for some luck, I said.

But don't you know any of the top men in some firm? he asked.

I know none, I said.

Even an MP? The one of your constituency? he asked.

No. That one is hard to see. It would take me months before seeing him. And perhaps not at all, I said.

How about your councillor? he asked.

I thought of those councillors. They are like ministers. To see them was another headache. They had bodyguards. Those youth wings. And if you saw them they would ask you where the vacancy was. And what would happen? Just another nut would be forwarded with a letter. I said No.

Any boss? he asked.

No, I said.

That is the trouble, he said. Unless you know one of the bosses it is just too hard. It was not like this during the white man's time. Corruption and tribalism have taken root everywhere.

Yeah. It is too unlucky for people like us who know no top people, I said. I wonder where the hell we are heading to. I think uhuru to a black man must be meaning something else.

Well, that is how it is. Let me go and see these people. I hope we will meet. He was ready to go when I stopped him.

Yeah. But before you go, I'm hard up. Help me with a bob, man, I begged.

He said nothing and only produced a five bob note and handed it to me.

I said thanks, and wished him prosperous. He left. I envied him in that khaki uniform and a big hat. Some guys were lucky, I thought. We discussed him and concluded that corruption had really taken root. Poor us, we said.

It was nearing noon and lunchtime when we said byes to each other, promising to meet in the afternoon or any time.

I took the same Commercial Street, leaving others to sleep their heads off in the afternoon sun. Among them the Legion Maria who was now preaching to the jobless. At Jogoo Road I was unable to

38

cross. There was a cycle competition. The competition of the workers racing to their ugali and sukuma, in Makongeni. Man, these folks can cycle, I thought. And they had a narrow margin so that if the leader happened to fall they would all land on each other.

I crossed the road after the old man, who seemed to be in no hurry. Perhaps he had cycled for the past ten years, so that all the medals he had won were patches piling up between his overalls, or sour, bruised-up thighs. I felt hungry. My throat was dry. I felt choking. I hurried to the Slums. I had some temptation to go to Burma but brushed that aside. I needed the Slums food. I met this pirate friend at the bridge, just where I met with Konga in the morning. He was buying some pineapples. Hello, man, he began.

Hello, how are you? I said.

Oh, not bad. Where from? he asked.

Down the Industrial Area, I said.

With me, I am just from Ziwani.

Where to? I asked.

To Kaloleni. I want to go and visit my friends of the Ashantis band, he said.

That is good, I said. As if he sensed it he told me to help myself to some piece. I helped myself and we said bye, hoping to meet each again.

At Katanga Base Hussein was nowhere to be seen, nor were the other car-washers. Perhaps they were all at Kwa Mama Kiosk. I left for Yasmin Hotel. There my friend Albi sold good dishes.

At the hotel Albi was not there, instead his brother was on duty. I ate and paid with the five bob note that I had been given. With the change in my pocket I headed for the Mairungi Stores. Back at Katanga Base I met Hussein, who already had the drug full green in his mouth.

How was the Labour? he asked.

Just like we left it. The population of the unemployed is growing from bad to worse, and if the government does not watch out, the situation will also grow into something worse, I explained.

That place should be done away with, said he. There is no point in it being there.

There is a slight chance of someone getting a job from there, I said.

Anyway let us just hope for the best, he said. We are still young.

Of course hope is always there with us, I said. We all hope for the best.

One day we won't be what we are now, that is, if we are still existing, he said.

That is right, I admitted. A change will of course come one day. That is a fact.

Every man has his day, he agreed. As they say every dog has its day.

Many who were once at the top are now at the bottom, I said.

Of course, said Hussein. And that is why I agree with the saying that it is better to start badly and end up a king.

One day all the boys here will not be what they are now. One day they will all eat bread and butter as long as they live, I said.

Yeah, agreed Hussein. All these car washings will be nothing but memories.

Yeah, I agreed. We will stop running from the law.

With the boredom of the place and with no business at the time I told Hussein that I was going back to the Labour to kill time there. He told me that he would just stay around. With that we parted.

On my way I wondered how whites get jobs. They never report at the labour, which is a bureau for all jobless. I concluded that they must be superior. How else could it be explained?

At the Labour I looked like a stranger. And that was because of miraa. The jobless looked at me as though I was mad. Some had never seen mairungi before. I chewed it and felt proud because of them looking at me. I ground the white sweet proudly. Made the place dirty with chewed sticks. They looked at me, but most of them started dozing due to heat and hunger. My two friends were not around. Well, Jerusalem was far. It was a long way for Hamisi.

40

And so was Kangemi for Ngugi. The sun was too much. Around four thirty, as the kingora, the siren of the G & R, indicated, I left the damn place. You would think I was coming from work the way I kept pace with these people from garages, offices and tarmac.

Back at Katanga Base I found Hussein busy on a black Benz. It had on it *CM*. Man, what a surprise. We never expected this type of car here. We only dealt with local men's cars. Managers, directors, thieves, taxis and what not. But Cabinet cars never. I approached him and asked who the damn hell the owner was? Before answering, he looked around to see where the owner was. Then he indicated to me with his mouth to a lady standing at the shops. I looked towards that direction. There stood with a coke bottle in her hands and black sunglasses on her face a woman in white slacks and a green polo-neck. Or her head a black wig. Down below, the leopard-skin sandals. Do the tyres, Hussein told me.

My mind still on the woman and thinking that she must have been fished from Caribbean seas, I went for the rags. Who was she for? I asked, bending over the tyres.

For the minister of love, sufferings and debts, he answered.

That meant he didn't know.

I don't know how we did this car. Sweat poured from our faces as if we had been in the field challenging Antao. When we finished, the lady came walking proudly and majestically. The walk of no care. The way she swayed her hips caused noises from the others. She inspected the car and got satisfaction. How much?

A pound, said Hussein.

With no objection she opened her leopard-skin handbag and from a smaller purse selected a new note from hundreds of others and handed it to Hussein. She got behind the wheel. Then, without us knowing why, she leaned out of the window and asked us our names.

I'm Hussein and this is Eddy, said Hussein.

I'm Zakia.

We nodded.

Thank you, she said, and roared the 280S away. She could drive. She left the topic behind about her. That was how we were when a woman with a figure happened to pass. It caused noises and

41

embarrassments. Towards evening we did three more cars. That was enough. We stored the washing-rags. We went to Amina's kiosk, Munyi's mama, and took mbaazi na mkate plus uji. Then when taking uji he began, So Labour is still the way we left it?

No change. I met my former schoolmate who now is a Wages Inspector who told me that unless I know one big fish in town I don't stand a chance of getting employment soon. That I should contact a minister, a councillor or a director who can give me a letter so that I can take it to the bosses. Just the everyday crap.

Corruption is leading us into a big deep hole that it will be hell to get out of. This brotherism and all that will land us into a grave, I am telling you, I said and went on: Mind you, at Labour also unless you know one of the officers there, there is a slim chance of being sent to a firm.

Well, to hell with work. We are working and our job is the best. You report when you want. Nobody to ask you why you were late and best of all we don't pay tax. No tax to the corrupted stealing nuts, he said. Not from us. We are not rich. It is on them.

They are the owners of millions in foreign banks, I said.

Yeah, when the volcano blows they will get it hard, said Hussein.

But where, man? The cheating nuts will book the first flights abroad. They will leave the beggers fighting and killing others like mad, I said.

To hell with them, cursed Hussein. He spat.

We paid the bill and left. Puffed and headed to Pumwani African Bar. Tonight we needed some busaa. In there the bar was full to the door. Tuneless songs went through the air. In a corner blew a juke-box. From it came 'Malaika' by Harry and Makeba, a composition by Fadhili. We pushed to the counter. There were no waiters or perhaps they were there but now everyone was a waiter. You could give them your money and get no drink. We were six, me, Hussein, Kadudu, Captain, Odongo and Jabbir. We carried our bottles around. Leaving a bottle on the table meant a sacrifice to somebody, those who fed from the remains in the bottles and glasses. They never bought. Those DDOs the Daily Drinking Officers. Captain was happy. But he had the disturbance of drying the pus from his forehead which kept on oozing from the crack there. That crack nearly killed him. He got it from Rwathias Gents Club. A waiter there threw him from three storeys high when he was drunk. He slept three weeks without coming to his senses. Kadudu was happy but not very, because his sugarmama in Jericho kicked him out to make room for her part-time boss who was coming from Germany. The owner of the house. He was not loved as he thought. The woman needed only a shoulder to cry on. And in turn she gave out her ageless happiness to Kadudu. In fact she was too old for Kadudu. We even sometimes wondered how they came to meet. They didn't make a loving picture of lovers. I pitied the man. He never knew that the woman he gave everything to and the bed he bought were being slept on by a mere down-at-heel full-of-lice cobbler. A car-washer slummer. Women!

Jabbir was trying to forget his troublesome dead girlfriend who was found dead in a hotel at Coast. I was trying to put some steam into myself. Then came a new song. It was by this crazy fellow in West Africa, the Kitch Doctor. A damn song. We wondered what the hell the world was coming to. Everyone's head is full of nothing but love. Young children too. Watch them in the Slums. You'll agree that the world is soon to come to an end. The children here know too much. A thing that our forefathers thought was meant for only them. A thing that brought the suffering of Adam into the world. Eve had the sweetest. When Adam tested it he forgot the promise that he made to God. It turned Adam into slavery. He had to work till all the hair on his head would leave a landing field for flies. Or a playfield for lice. Adam was silly. Instead of mangoes, oranges and apples he liked the kiss. Shit. Causing a man to work, work and work to feed the glutton wife. In fact any job is slavery. Be it presidency, stealing or begging and washing cars. Without it you are dead. You will go to hell. It was a rope around your neck. A white man's rope. Every day it tightened a bit. Every day you are getting worn out but you don't know. Without it you'll eat shit. Then your nails. When they are finished *shauri yako*, it is up to you. You eat to live, not live to eat. We watched the reactions of the slobs. Some tried to dance. Then we came to rest our eyes on these two couples. One, the lady was this Kadogo. She had a tooth

43

missing in the upper row, leaving a nice gap for a tongue to pass when kissing. Too bad the slob she was with didn't know about kisses. She knew. Two years back she was one of the queens here. When she was Pancho's. But since she took to drinking she's so much worn out. Women wear out so fast. The way they were acting would make you think differently. The guy wanted her. We drained the stuff. It wasn't good. Too cold. Out we marched. The bar was good for old boozers. Not us.

I haven't felt a thing, complained Odongo. And that was because he was a Changaa addict.

Me, too. That was Captain.

And Kadudu added: In fact the stuff was poor.

So where to? I asked.

To Njoki's, Kadudu proposed.

Yeah, to Njoki's, agreed Odongo and Jabbir.

No, we opposed. Me and Captain. Hussein too supported us. To Mama Atieno, we said.

Okay, we all agreed. To Mama Atieno. We headed there. On reaching there we found some of the boys had been there. Burma group. We took a full glass each. We left. Outside, the stuff took stimulation. The blasts of the drunks started. We forgot that the bobbies were around rounding up drunks. Whether drunk or not. They were after the bribe. We passed between the dark alleys. The two-shilling tarts thought we were for them. At the sight of one I approached her and began the usual way. *Habari?* How are you?

Fine. How are you?

Fine. Is there a chance? I asked.

She sensed it. The Changaa smell. That was final. She said, No. A good lie, because the room was not occupied. There was nobody. And of course they admitted no drunk.

I said, Goodbye then.

Bye, she shot at me, while I followed the trail of the others who were ahead disturbing those they found standing at their doors. Waiting.

We came to Njoki's place. Out there in this kiosk a tape-recorder was playing some taarabs songs. In it mbaazi na mkate was sold.

44

And so was the kahawa. Slummers sat in there chewing gatty. *Shkamooni jamaa*, we greeted them.

Marhaba maalims, they answered.

We went in. In there we met Sammy, Njirose, Burma, Yossa, Abbasi and Ally. Sammy looked too drunk. He was dozing his head off. Some trail of saliva to his chest. Beside him on the bed were four bastards, the products of Mohammed when he was a false husband to this bitch. He divorced her and got married to a true wife, abandoning all the children to her to feed. He emigrated to Kariobangi. That is how this place was. A wise guy didn't marry here; I mean, a lady from the Slums. That is why so many bastards are found here. The ladies know too much.

Shkamoo? Njoki was greeted.

Marhaba. Fine, she said.

Habari za kushinda? How was the day? we asked.

Fine, she said. Yes? For the order? she said.

One shilling each, we said.

All of you? she asked.

Yes, we answered.

Then my voice awoke Sammy. Hey, Eddy, one on you.

I told Njoki to give it him. These two guys were funny. I mean Sammy and Abbasi. They shared this woman Njoki. And they both knew it. Each one had his time. Abbasi was now the father of all those four bastards. And that was because the four had been instructed to call him father. And so they called him. It was not strange or funny. It was serious. We gulped the pombe in one gulp. It was an illegal brew. Out we marched. But we didn't get far. At the main gate we met with them, the flatfeet or bobbies or cops, njako or police or makarai or utumishi kwa wote. Call them anything. Even plain robbers. Or clubbers. They had on sombreros. Mud-boots and kabutis. Our blood ran cold. This mud-house plot had no back door. They shone the torch on us. Stop, they commanded.

We stood.

Drunks? they asked.

No. We said. A stupid lie. These guys smelled mouths. They did it.

Ooooh. You have drunk Changaa.

We said nothing. We had betrayed ourselves.

You go, they ordered Hussein. He had only the slight smell of busaa. He must be lucky. Run and don't look back. He ran.

Man. What bad luck, I thought. Whenever the slummers enjoy their hard-earned mapeni cents, it was always interfered with. Garbage. This was garbage shit. Then they produced handcuffs. The automatic shiny China-made. Too bad for us. Then came Brazze. He was shouting his words off through his mouth. *Watu yote kama satan*. All people are devil-like. The cops heard him. He was knocking passers-by. *Watu yote kama satan*, he repeated. The cops thought that he was referring to them because we laughed when we heard him. Two challenged him. *Kuja hapa*, come here, they roared at him. He paid no attention. He repeated his words. They landed on him. Too bad for them. They underrated him. They must be new around there. Wrestling started. The third one joined them. We would have escaped but for these Chinese imports. We watched the wrestling, while four of them guarded us. They threw him down. That way they did it. One kicked him in the ribs. Again another. What brutality. One stepped on his head. They pulled him up. A club landed on his back. Merciless brutes. Nincompoops. Wanyama, I thought.

Brazze spat in the face of one.

It landed on him. On the cheeks. The never-play-with-the law slap.

We watched it calmly. Passers-by avoided coming near. Only their curses could be heard as they left.

Then began the march to the chief's camp. Brazze gave them such a hard time they didn't bother to go in. They would have fished plenty. With our bangles we marched. Brazze was all alone. We walked. At the Memorial Hall like a flash Brazze took to his heels. With the bangles on. This nut could run. They went after him. Three of them. The rest still guarded us. What was wrong today? They didn't want anything today? From Njoki's place we had been trying to seduce them with bribes, but all in vain. You are very rude, was all they told us. And that was all because of Black Christ, this Brazze. Shit. At the chief's camp they bundled

46

us all into the chief's room. We sat on the floor. They threatened to smash our heads if we didn't tell them who the guy was who ran with the cuffs. If they didn't get him. We waited. Waited. Then came the nuts. Empty-handed. No Brazze. No bangles. Man, if somebody had told me that police could beat a guy half to death I wouldn't have believed it. They were the people to maintain order and peace. How wrong? The beating started. No joke. These cops could beat. They must have trained also in how to beat a raia, a citizen. A drunkard matataless raia. They beat us. The worst fell on Odongo. They roughed him up, half to death. Who knows the fellow who escaped? they asked.

We kept mum.

Who knows him? they repeated.

We kept mum. If they hadn't beaten Odongo that way we would have had second thoughts. But now? Never.

Whoever tells will go.

We kept quiet.

Okay, you will get it again. We will beat you up.

Go on, said Jabbir. Kill us if you want. We won't tell. He got it. Bah.

Don't you know that fellow ran away with the government's property? they asked.

So what? asked Jabbir. Couldn't you run?

They now looked helpless. They just looked at us. Let's leave them, said one.

It's no use. Perhaps he was trying to be nice or something, when helpless. That is how they are. When completely helpless you feel mercy on them. Even a thief is better. You could see his guilt. Openly. If you want to prove it steal a cop's baton or whistle. Worst of all the crown. Hide the crown. Then watch his face. He will permit you to have his wife.

We said nothing. We waited for the recovery of Odongo. God. They had roughed this guy. Then they rang for the 999 Mariamu from Shauri Moyo. The Man-cage. More of the drunkards joined us. Some quite as sober as a judge, if a judge is ever sober. When the van came we were all sober. Those who got the beating.

47

Odongo was snoring. We got into it. Odongo was thrown in like a sack full of salt.

Man, do you know that the night is very long when you don't sleep wink? And especially in a cell? The night was long.

In the morning we were all bundled into the van with only one file. Four police accompanied us to Makadara, the famous court for the drunks and domestic women cases. And the mimba pregnancy cases. I was once here on that type of a case. I impregnated Wamboi during our primary education, five years back.

At Makadara, we entered the big cage of a zoo. The barbed wire all around us. Just like the Gestapo. We were animals. Men in a zoo. I thought of Sebastian the monkey in the cage at the National Park. They better set that guy free. He needs freedom. Freedom to enjoy his world. There is no point of fighting for liberation and keeping others in cages for money. This thought always came to me whenever I was brought here. Since the kanyaga cases. Trespassings. Man. A man's freedom is a great thing. Just be free. Don't be rich or anything. Just be left alone to do your own thing. To move.

Then the cases started. More than ten people were called. The charge was read to them. Last night you were found drunk and misbehaving in public.

Yes or no? asked the judge with hungover eyes.

If you said no you were remanded for two weeks. If you said yes you might be fined anything. Even fifty cents. And if you failed to pay the fine you got three weeks. So yes was better. Don't argue.

Then it happened in the history of Makadara for the first time. Two prominent people were among us. It made everyone laugh. A Kibera magistrate was among us. He had been rounded up somewhere in the Slums. Those who got him perhaps never knew who he was. But that is what I say. A law is a law. Nobody is above the law. So in Kibera there was no magistrate. They rang from there to check if this magistrate was here. He was a drinker, they all knew. He got fined fifty bob. At the door waiting for him was a Thames to take him to Kibera. He went.

48

Then came the case of this minister. He has not been a drinker all his life. But he was found also in the Slums. The magistrate could not believe himself. He asked the reasons for this minister being in the filthy corrupted Slums?

I'm a mwananchi, a citizen. I went there like anybody else, he answered.

For the two-shilling tarts? asked the judge.

Yeah. And also for drinking, answered the minister, rudely.

So you misbehaved in public also?

I don't know if I did. I was drunk.

One hundred and fifty. You top people should keep away from such filthy places. You must set good examples to those local maskinis. He paid the fine and left people wondering about him.

Then it came to us. Ten or fifteen of us were called. The magistrate could not even see the faces of the others. He was the same one as I had during my case with Wamboi. He still recalled my face because during the case I was so bold. I don't know where I got all the courage from. I asked Wamboi only one question and she couldn't answer or it put her out. I asked her: Do you remember that after every kiss I had from you I gave you a shilling for mangoes?

She said, Yes.

That finished the whole case. The magistrate termed her a tramp.

He read the charge to us. Then he smiled. Among us was an old man whose face was familiar to the magistrate. The magistrate laughed his head off. That old boozer saved us. We were fined anything that we had in our pockets. We paid.

Out, we met Hussein. Hey, men, you are out?

Yeah.

How much did they fine you?

Thirty cents.

No joke?

No joke.

You must be lucky.

Oh yeah, we are, we all said.

Brazze got away with the cuffs, he said.

Yeah. How did it all go? we asked in unison.

We got them removed. It was a hard job. They hurt him on the wrist.

He is a nut. He got us beaten, complained Odongo.

It was funny the way he dodged them. Those cops must be new around, Hussein explained. They didn't know that there are doors at the back of the plots. They looked silly the way they looked around for him.

We talked on our way to the bus stop at Bahati. We admired the ladies at this Huruma boarding school. It reminded me of my former lady. Lady Bongsteel. A nut with a bushy beard pinched her without my knowledge. It is a great misfortune to have a beautiful girl who loves you while you have no job and she is in trouble. When you can't even afford to buy her knickers. When you can't even afford to take her out to the flicks, movies. Too bad when you can't even afford to buy her a coke, in the boogy. She will be pinched. The playboys are there with money to fool them with. When things turn sour, after she has been used, that was when she will think of you. By then she is worn out. She is scrap. Second hand. I remembered, when she came and poured out all her tears, that she never knew it could be what it turned out to be.

Back in the Slums we headed to the Riatha Hotel. We were feeling too damn hungry. In the morning that tea at the police station was too cold for any sweetness, and so were the scones. From there we took to Katanga.

At Base the main topic of the day was the story about Brazze's escape with the bangles. Pingu. Brazze himself was not around. Perhaps he was hiding in that church at Santa Maria. Kanisani Mbanyo. Odongo went to nurse his ribs at his part-time woman's Chimio. They were the other funny couple here. That Chimio woman was a mother of six. Three big ripe daughters and three young sons. The first four she got with her former husband who kicked her out because of secret affairs she was having around with some young chaps. Odongo was the best. She took to Odongo. She got a room and all her four moved in. Two of her sons are Odongo's products. But sometimes Odongo doesn't sleep there. That

50

happens when Chimio has a slob for a night from whom she would get a pound for the feed of her children. Plus beer. This we always knew when he came to sleep in the ruins. So, the bangle story went on. It was a nice change because here at Katanga Base the stories are the same every day. It is always a repetition of yesterday and yesterday and how a drunk bitch was raped. That was 'Combine'.

Then business started. That cut out the stories. Everyone worked. Then towards evening in rolled this white Ford. In it Phillip. A cool guy. He talked little. Quite innocent. With the appearance of a tough nut. Man, if somebody told you that this nut is a crook you perhaps would have betted your life. He looked an executive. No difference from Bilali. His car was never washed by anybody else. It was only for Burma and Uha. The boot was never opened. The boys feared his character. One day he brought this car here for washing. He had left his fags in the glove compartment. Rex, three packets. Then by beautiful luck Hussein was seen taking one without his permission. He came, uttered no word. He gave Hussein the three packets. He went and bought a ten-cents packet. That was not enough. Another time he came again. He had bought a newspaper. I made the mistake. He found me looking at the vacancies' column. He said nothing. He went and bought another. When driving off he called me and told me to take the paper. Those two things were enough for us to know what type of a character he was. We suspected him. And that was because of his movements. We played nosy and came to find out all about him. He was a bank robber.

So when this Ford rolled in we knew where it had been. On a mission. It had this red dust. Then rolled in another green one but not a Ford. This one is new around here. We knew all the car number-plates which come here. All the customers. This one was new. It was the first time for it to appear here. So I approached it. It was a small Colt with another CM plate on it. This was strange. Last time it was that Benz and now this Colt. Perhaps these guys want to see the Slums to recommend their demolition. When I reached him I said, *Jambo Mheshimiwa*. Hello, your honour.

Hello, how are you? he asked.

Mzuri Mheshimiwa. Fine, your honour. Then he explained that his Colt needed a wash. I went for water and my rags. On coming back expecting him to be out I got a surprise. He had wound up all the windows and was inside reading a big-volumed book. On the back seat were more of these big volumes. Well, I decided, if you want it that way you will get it that way. After all it reduces the washing of rags and the roof. When I had finished I knocked three times before he looked up. I indicated to him that it was finished. He pulled down the window and asked how much. Fifteen, I said.

He paid and didn't bother to come out to check. He drove off. I watched him going. I smiled.

When he had gone I called the others and told them to guess who that damn bald-headed man was. His face appeared familiar to some. We had seen it so many times in newspapers in the reports about Parliament. They couldn't guess. Only that we had seen his face in the papers. Too bad Burma was not around. He would have got it. Then I told them. It was that famous man of the People's Declaration. That man who caused some troubles in the River Valley, Mr Ngumi. The boys wondered. They wanted to see him personally. Then the talk started on him, about his fame. His objections to land distribution to other tribes from other areas. A character.

With the balance that I had from the two pounds and the fifteen shillings, I thought of having a change in my Lee. I told Hussein that I was going to Darajani to look for some cheap trousers. Mine were now worn out so that I didn't feel comfortable in them. I ran to Darajani. There I got corduroys for a pound and some cheap brown army tennis shoes. Those would do. On my way back I branched off to Bondeni toilet-bathrooms. I needed a wash before putting on my new outfit. I washed. I changed, wrapping beautifully in the paper the Y-front with the resident lice in it. I left it on the wall for some poor slob to feel happy when he found it. He would be surprised. He wouldn't pick things up again. As for the safaris, I dropped them into the trench. The pipe flowing with water and shit would pull them along. Coming out of the

52

bathroom I met with this lady. A student at Khalsa. I had watched her so many times dropping off at the bus stop and going on foot between the wrecks without interest. Sometimes our eyes had met and I had seen her hiding the secret smile. Sometimes we had even booed at her with her friend Wanjiko. You would mistake them for sisters. And so she began. Hello, she said.

Hello, I said.

She stopped. I stopped. I never expected this. After all, to a down-at-heel, mere cobbler car washer.

Are you Eddy? she asked.

What if I am? A reaction I like to have when a woman asks my name. It makes me proud. You never know how much they have talked about you.

I'm only asking you, she said.

How did you come to know my name? I asked.

It is not strange, is it? she asked.

It is, I said.

How? she asked.

I don't know how but it is strange that you know my name when I don't know yours, I said.

I'm Lizzy, she explained.

Thank you, but who introduced my name to you? I asked.

You are known. I asked a small boy and he told me, she said.

Then you are all wrong, I said.

Why? she asked.

Because my name is not Eddy, I said.

What is your name then? she asked.

Chura, I said.

Don't be funny, she replied.

Sorry if I am. But that is my real name and I'm proud to have it, I said.

That made her laugh. A phony laugh. It was not funny or fit to cause laughter.

You are cheating, she said.

Prove it, I said.

I can't, but you are Eddy, she said.

Eddy Chura, I added.

Now I know, she said.

Okay, now you know, but why? I asked.

I just wanted to know.

Why did you? I asked.

I'm interested. Or I was interested, she said.

Then jump up for joy, I said.

See, I'm jumping. She did.

You're mad, I said.

I'm not, she replied.

Well, I must be going 'cause I think you're happy now, I said.

Will you come?

Goodness. Where?

I want to see you, she explained.

What about?

Come and I'll tell you, she replied.

Where? I asked.

Where should we meet? I mean where can I meet you? she asked.

Say some place, I said.

Let's meet at Mfereji wa Dhambi.

At what time? I asked.

Around eight.

Okay. I'll come, I said.

See you then, she finished. We parted.

At Katanga Base I found the boys listening to Omar's radio. It was a commercial station. I joined them. Then Suleiman started the argument. It was on the broadcasters of Tanzania and ours. He claimed that those nuts knew better than ours. The boys agreed with him. Kesho and Shosho objected. They argued. Kesho and Shosho were high because of gabba. At seven thirty we took supper. Mbaazi na mkate. Uji to wash it down. At Mama Atieno's we took it hurriedly in one gulp. That for 'kuvunja kichwa' or 'kutupa kwa roho' or 'up mara moja'. At a few minutes past eight I was at Mfereji wa Dhambi. At first I didn't see her. She was in a black kabuti. Then she hissed to me. I joined her and we took a stroll. From Mfereji wa Dhambi we took Meru Road towards Maternity. Okay, I said. Tell me.

What? she asked.

You wanted to see me.

Well I have seen you, she replied.

Is that the only thing you wanted? I asked.

Yeah.

Well I think I better go then, I said.

No, she said.

What do you mean?

I mean no, she said.

Well you have seen the thing you wanted, I said.

Yeah, but you are not going, she said.

Now what is your hide and seek game? I asked.

Guess.

I can't.

Why?

I failed guessing in my examination. In my KAPE, I said.

That made her laugh. Then . . . I never thought you were so funny, she said.

I don't think I am. It is only you who is making me look a clown, I said.

Why? she asked.

Your laughter. I don't see any reason for it, I said.

You are funny, she said.

Spare that and give me a distinction instead, I said.

I give it you, she said.

Thank you for that honour, but now tell me or I'll go, I said.

Why are you so blind? she asked.

I'm not.

Then you better start seeing from now, she said.

Then we came to this Masandukuni Bar. The boys, among them Franco, Dan, Saidi, Mwaura, Ally, Ahmed, Njirose and Yossa, were there having beer. This to kill off the stink of cham. You would think that they had taken a crate each. And that was why this brew was termed illegal. If put in the market the beer wouldn't have any market. Too good for a quick drunk. A deadly stimulator.

55

A kill-me-quick. If I was alone I would have been there but this mongrel of a female was with me. I didn't like taking a woman to such places. I mean where money is concerned. I'm a jealous member of parliament. The House of Jealousy. I always felt my intestines coiling when I imagined how that bushy bearded bagger was with Zeituni. So I avoided the place. We passed it. At the junction of this Lumbwa Road we took the road towards Ziwani. At the bus stage I told her how once some crooks robbed me of my money.

It was one Sunday we went to Ziwani. I was with my friend Machunjuru Oruka. We went to this Ziwani busaa party. It was a nice party I had never attended before. An open air party. No invitation cards. It was held beside the road opposite the Child Maternity. We boozed up, watching the passers-by in buses and on foot. No glasses. Only the big Kimbo tins. From morning to evening. Then Oruka got hijacked by this mother popcorn, Mbithe. I never saw him again. When I got fed up with waiting for him and with enough uji of this busaa, I staggered back. That was around eight. Then at this bus stop because there are no lights here right up from Starehe I met with them. At first I thought that they were waiting for a bus. God. How mistaken I was. Three of them. A glittering panga was produced from inside the kabuti. The nut held me by the neck while the two conducted their search into my pockets. Money plus the ID went. I don't know where they went to display it. That made her announce, Maskini. I smiled inwardly. I now held her close. She rested her head on my shoulder. Swine, cheating fool, I cursed her. You are all the same. You like cheating. At Ziwani Field we got in. Still holding each other. We sat under these inscriptions 'Umeme Club'. I remarked how once I was a good winger. Then started the kisses and fondlings.

Whoever said that getting into a habit is easy and getting out is hard had some guts to spill. Hussein's parents were not rich. In short, they were poor. During the Emergency troubles and Mau Mau when every Kikuyu needed a pass to come into the city, they were living at Bahati. They were a family of four. Mother, father, he and his sister, Asha. Who at the moment is roaming the streets of Nairobi as a tart. Malaya. His father was in the business of selling chupa na debe. Buying and selling the bottles and tins. Youngsters used to run behind him repeating after him chupa na debe, chupa na debe. And so he was famous. So one night when things grew hot and so did the Mau Mau, he was picked up. They raided the houses.

Luckily Hussein's mother was in a neighbour's house. Hussein and Asha were considered to be too young. They took him. This was on the ground that he was suspected to be helping the Mau Mau. That those bottles he was buying were used in storing the Muma. The Oath. A mixture of blood, human blood, dogs' and cats', and all kinds of shit. But it was all a lie. It was a neighbour who gave out a false accusation. A fellow tribesman. Away they took him. And that included some other suspects. They took him to Makongeni Police Station and to the field. From there to Majengo around the War Memorial which had at that time barbed wire like the Gestapo. They were squeezed into the small room which nowadays is a store. From there they were bundled into a big lorry and transported to detention camps. First to Maralal, then Kapenguria and on to Lodwar. That was the last of him. They heard no more of him for some years to come. As for the mother and the sister, they shifted from Bahati to here in the Slums. Plus Hussein. They turned into Muslims. Njeri, the mother, changed her name to Mamu. Asha for Wangoi and Hussein for Mwangi. And that's why Hussein doesn't believe in the Muslim faith. He is a false Muslim. And so are many here.

Then one day a bad fate fell on the mother. It was a sunny morning and, as is a habit of the women in the Slums, she was plaiting a fellow woman's hair with only a khanga wrapped around her breast. She had nothing on underneath. Then the crooked Hussein hit the young daughter of a neighbour. That started it. The mother of the girl slapped Hussein three hard blows on the cheek. Hussein's mother felt it in her heart. She got up and started the stupid abuse song which in the Slums is like 'good morning'. Abuse in the Slums is like 'Hellos'. Like saying good morning to a friend. Both sexes. Young and old. So began the fight of the mothers. They fought. Hussein's mother was too strong for the other one. Her khanga fell off. That aroused laughter in the watchers. The Slums people were very silly. They lived to enjoy such things. Those naked scenes. While she bent to pick it up, the other one ran into her house. When she came out she had a small tin. You would have thought that the contents were water. And that perhaps she was going to the toilet. That is because the Muslims carry tins with them to the toilets. Or perhaps the onlookers thought that she was going to pour the shit inside on Hussein's mother. In the Slums people don't go to toilets at night. They shit in tins, pouring it out to the morning. Into the trenches. But what was in that tin was not water for toilet purposes. It was acid. She emptied it all on the face of Hussein's mama. It caused her blindness. It caused the end of her business that she was carrying on to pay the school fees for both Hussein and Asha. Their aunt who came to help in it from Gatito stole the profit. By then Hussein was in form four at City High School and Asha in form three at Kenya Girls'. The mother turned to begging. With Asha's bastard on her back.

At school, Asha was very good in her studies. She topped the class at the end of every term. She had got a sponsorship to that school after passing her KAPE with distinction. In Kenya Girls' she was the only girl from the filthy African slums. All her mates were daughters of Black Europeans. Daughters of ministers, directors and general managers who have only seen pictures of the slums and swear that such places don't exist in Nairobi. They would stick a finger into their mouths and lick them, pointing to the ground and swearing that such places were only found in China and America. That is because they don't have time to walk around in our slums to see what type of life goes on there. They were born in the bush trees of Milimani, Lavington Green, Kileleshwa and such where a common man can never think of living. Places where a poor common man can never even go for a walk. So many dogs are around to bark them away. Blacks are the worst racists. Imagine, a black man who doesn't want a fellow black. Silly.

In the places where they live you will find *Mbwa Kali*, 'Hawkers are not allowed' signs. These are to keep the common man away. He is unwanted in their society. Simply because he hasn't the qualifications. He doesn't have a Benz. And he is not a Chairman. He was born a beggar and so he should remain a beggar till his dying day. He belongs to the slums of Mathare Valley, Santa Maria, along the Nairobi river, Makaburini and anywhere far from the city. These slums should even be got rid of.

So in her class she topped the others. She was attentive to her studies. The black Europeans in turn enjoyed the weekend dances. The Boogies. Where they drank, puffed and spent the time out with their boys. They puffed the bhang too. Never cared. They danced at Starlight, Acadia, Camay, Hallians, killing it out at 1900 Bar. The next day and on Monday, they gossiped about it. In the daytime and even more in the dormitories at night. All the time Asha listened. Finally she one day attempted to join them. A thing they had longed for. And which ended Asha's schooling.

It was one Saturday afternoon when a classmate told her that there was a party in the evening at one of their friends'. That it would be after they had come from the boogy. That afternoon each one had on her best. The one preserved for such an occasion. From Kenya Girls' they went to drop in at Icelands. There they didn't find the group they were looking for. They entered Exotica. There they were entertained with some cold coke. They were six in number. They met three of the boys they were looking for. They accompanied each other to Pop-In. There they bought the dope. And all the time Asha was feeling odd girl out. She hadn't found a boy. The others were looking for their boys. Having puffed the dope, they all shot off to Acadia. Too bad for Asha. It was her first experience. She started laughing unnecessarily. Any slight thing made her laugh. At Acadia the boogy went on. They danced. Asha danced but with the wrong timing, laughing at any boy who passed by. Finally she found herself in the hands of one of the crooked gangs. The Sun Valley Gang. They danced. The chap, who happened to be Emmu and from the Slums, but who didn't know who Asha was, cheated her with all the crap a crook would give a new find. Then it came to the time that the boogy was coming to an end. Asha, who had no experience of whisky, was cheated into drinking it. She didn't know that an Aspro tablet had been dropped into it. In a gulp she drained it. It took its effect. When she woke the next day she found that she could not walk properly. She didn't know that ten of the Sun Valleys had broken her hymen. It took her a week to get back a proper walk. She never returned to school. She got pregnant. That baby she left with her mother and took to the streets, where she was parading now. Hussein went on and finished school. He got a third grade.

So when their mother turned blind she got into begging. With the bastard on her back. She started waiting for people on the near side road. When you passed nearby she clung on to you and begged you to lead her into town. In town she begged along Government Road and Kimathi Street. Ending seated at Woolworth opposite New Stanley. She did this for some days. One day another cheating crook told her that he was going the same route as her. To the Slums. The nut took her to the slums of Makaburini. They drank her money. Raped her. The next day she was found at the Race Course Bridge, face downwards and the bastard with her. Both dead. That began Hussein sleeping in the old worn-out scraps of cars in the Slums. We met here five years back.

When we met we were desperate. We had no way to eat. We presented ourselves at Labour every day without success. We blew two years, entering every office. At last we got fed up. We entered into the world of playing Three Cards with some experienced crooks. We played it on streets and beside footpaths. To women on their ways to markets. We didn't like losing. In that game we were guards. I stood at one end and Hussein at the other. This for security purposes. And also because we did not know how to mix the cards. At the sight of a suspected cop we had to whistle. We gave it up when the cops got to be hard to recognise in plain clothes. We switched to shop-lifting.

We would enter a shop in a group of four or five. We would confuse the shop attendants by asking for this and that, no, not that one, the one behind it, and what was the price? We would then leave on the pretext that it was very dear. They never knew that we had picked up some stuff free. We sold the things here. At a cheap price. The money was spent with these cheating Swahili women. They only love you when you have money, otherwise you can get lost. We dropped this shop-lifting when the Asians got

60

familiar with our faces and habits. And also because three of us got seven years with strokes. Now being desperate we got into picking pockets. This at bus stops. Too bad if once you were a victim to us. Forgive me. We operated along the stops at OTC, opposite Tusker, Hilton, Ambassadeur and all the major stops. We would board a bus to any destination, squeezing and pushing people and standing at the stairs. All that while picking pockets. We stopped doing this when they caught us at it. They applied Public Justice to us. Beatings. They pushed me through the Emergency Door. While the bus was on the move. I fractured a small finger. Hussein fractured an arm. From that world we joined forging. Cheques. We would steal an already cashed one and study it. Or sometimes bribe a messenger in a bank to steal one for us. Then we would retire to practise forging it. I was good at that. Once qualified we bribed for the balance statement of an intended victim. We signed a cheque for it. The money was spent in the same way. Women and drinking. When Shorty got fourteen and twenty-four strokes, that was the end of it. From that we went on to selling water and then to the present legal car-washing.

3

It was Saturday afternoon when we were doing nothing, this CM Benz pulled up. The same lady in it. Man, today she was different. I mean in her get-up. She had on white slacks and a red pullover. No joke, this tart know how to fashion. Sunglasses where they were last time. Her feet in slippers. I approached her. Hello memsahib, I said.

Oh. Hullo. How are you? she asked.

Not bad, I said.

That's good. I want it washed and everything done, she said.

That will be done, I said. I wondered where this monkey Hussein was.

Where is your mate? she asked.

Gone to the toilet, I lied.

Will you wash it alone? she asked.

Yes, I said.

Ain't it a hard job? she asked.

No. We're used to it, I said.

She said nothing more. She went and stood under this tree near the shop. I called for water and started. Kaballo did the tyres. The boys started talking in a funny tone. That was all about her. They admired her hips. Wishing for a night with her. Monkeys, I said.

When we had finished it, she inspected it, got inside and told me to get in on the other side. That was like a bomb in my face. I stood looking at her transfixed. Get in, she repeated.

I looked at my feet and didn't know whether to get in or not. She smiled and leaned over to open the door. What I didn't know was that the others were watching us. Then Mayanja shouted over that I should enter without worrying. *Ingia Mazee, usijali*. Burma repeated it. I got in. She reversed and we rolled off. She told me that she wanted to take a drive around the Slums. And that I was to be her guide.

She told me that she had heard a lot about the place and had never had a chance to know it better. That eased my tension. All the time I was wondering to myself what this woman was really after. We took the Digo Road and I showed her our butcheries. Hanging at the doors, the matumbo meat. Flies swarming around the carcasses. You would have thought they were towels for sale. They were a sight to please the eyes. Seing them caused some wrinkles to form on her face. She asked, Are they edible?

Yeah. They are cheap. Good boiling and the germs die. The sight didn't please her. We branched at this junction towards Shauri Moyo. I showed her the Women's Community. I told her that dyeing was taught there. I pointed out the STC. That is the VD clinic. And I added that it was the best place for that cure.

Is that because of the two-shilling tarts? she asked.

Well, I think so. Waziba are many here, I said.

Have you entered them? she asked.

Yeah. I am not married yet and they are for that purpose, I said.

How do they, I mean how do you approach them? she asked.

That is easy. You don't have to be drunk. If you are drunk they won't agree, I said.

Eh? She remarked.

Yeah, I said.

And then? she asked.

You say, How are you? Fine, she answers. You ask, Any chance? Then if there is, which of course there must be if she is not in her period, you go in, I said.

That's all? she asked.

Yeah.

That's too much of a job, she remarked.

Not to them. They're used to it. It is their source of income. Bosses too come here. Even some ministers get theirs here. They always come at night, park their cars at a distance. That annoyed her. Aren't they infectious? she asked.

63

Not likely. Perhaps at the end of the month, when the hungry wolves with the itchy money in their pockets don't give them time to wash. You will see those people jumping like frogs over the shit without taking any care. It is a funny place at the end of the month when they all come. Even if it is raining. They are like beasts. You will hear them cursing, some of them complaining because they have found the one they wanted with somebody else. You will see them drying the sweat from their faces. It was very funny, I told her. You would laugh to death the way they are knocking and crossing each other.

I pointed to some of them sitting at the doorsteps. Like those, I said.

We drove. Took this Nandi Street. I showed her the toilets and explained that in the Slums here we bathe in the toilets. At night time we don't go to the toilets. I showed her the tins drying along the trenches. The shits are poured out in the morning. She shook her head. Along this road we passed these pickpockets. They were the Kondos who had escaped from Uganda. They were without business now because the month was not ended yet. Then at the end of this Nandi Street we came to a stop at these slums of Santa Maria. Some of them are the Kidingwa dancers, Akamba dancers, entertainers. That one there is a Peace-Corps white woman, I pointed out. She is under that tree teaching those children how to read. We don't know where she came from. Behind them is the Kajificheni building. And behind it is the newly built Biafra Estate. We drove on.

We took this Hamilton Street. On my right I pointed to the new houses of the New Pumwani or California estate. We drove on slowly. I told her to branch left on to this Kikuyu Street. The dust was blowing on us. I showed her the Bangla Desh Kiosk. I pointed out to her the owner, a handicapped fellow. He was seated on his wheelchair. Behind the counter was the wife. Coming along in a good file the debes, waiting for water. I saw Rehema with her recently born bastard. These slum girls. I wondered what future they were heading to. They play the game which is their mothers' business. In return . . . bastards. Some have more than four. All with different fathers. The love here was too free. It was spoiling

64

their lives and shortening them. It was an inheritance from their mothers and grannies. I pointed to one of them and explained the corruption of women here to her. That girl is not yet sixteen but was a mother now. I pointed to this door marked 'College'. I lied about that, saying it was a college for two-shilling tarts.

Is it? she asked.

Yeah. That is where they are taught all the business. I pointed to Willy busy on cars. He is a mechanic. Mwai was busy cheating his friends. We stopped and parked the big car behind a trailer. She bought a pair of sandals and we carried them with us. Then she asked me why I was not chewing miraa today.

I lied, telling her I didn't have any cash.

Do you want some? she asked.

Yeah, I said.

Let's go and buy some. I will pay for it for you. We approached one of the stalls of this Abaite, Meru Mairungi Store. We bargained and bought two kilos. Four bundles. We took to the alleys. Skipping over the decoration of human shit left by both young and old in our walk. Behind the mud-houses. She spat out her sweet saliva. I showed her the bed for love in one of the mzibas' houses. Each house had two beds. The small one was the one for business. The well-made one was for her and her false husband. We moved on. Along our path in a trench were lined up five youngsters. Two girls and three boys. One of the girls was crying. She hated that sight. She decided that we should go back to our car.

We drove on till we came to stop at the Memorial Hall. I told her that from this hall sprang the country's top boxers, Olulu, Thega, Ali Juma, Attan and many more who have represented the country at the Olympics and the Commonwealth Games. I showed her the mechanics at Katanga, Hamisi and Juma. The chief's camp too. That is all, I said.

Thanks a lot. But tell me. What do you do? I mean what work do you do?

I have no work, I answered.

Why? she asked.

Well, I haven't found a job yet, I said.

Have you really looked? she asked.

65

Yeah. I have walked into every office but no luck, I said.

Did you do your school certificate? she asked.

Yeah, I said.

When? she asked.

Five years back, I said.

My God. Do you really mean that you have been without a job for five years?

That is it, I said.

That is too much, she remarked.

Well the day hasn't come, I said.

My God. I just can't believe it, she said.

Well, you have to. You see, these people at the top don't know what sort of life a common man leads in the Slums. And that is why you can't believe it. There is so much corruption in the country that we slummers don't know where the hell we are heading to, I said.

And how about your parents? she asked.

That killed me.

Dead. They died in an accident, I said.

When? she asked

Some years back, I said

Any of your family left? she asked.

Yes, but we are all scattered. One in the Forces, one in the slums of Mathare Valley, another in Kibera, an eloped sister in Kariobangi selling changaa and all that. No good life, I explained.

And where do you live? she asked. That hurt me.

Right there in the wrecks of all those cars, I said, and pointed them out.

You mean you sleep in them? She was surprised.

That's it. Better there than along River Road. Sometimes when it is very cold and rainy and the police are out for us, we jump out and go into the mosque. We are out in the early hours, I explained.

And how about the rest of them? She pointed out the boys.

All in the same category, just as you see them.

And which is yours? she asked.

66

That white one. The one with sacks on its windows as curtains.

I'm very sorry, she said, and her face proved it.

Don't worry. It is how people are born. We are not all born the same, I replied.

And suppose I get a place for you, will you agree? she asked.

Yeah, I will, I said.

I will try my best for you. Here, take this. She handed me a fifty-shilling note. You can do anything you like with it, she said.

Thanks, madam, I said.

It's O.K. And with that she drove her Benz off. What a lucky afternoon, I thought.

Back at Base I found Hussein, Jabbir and Mayanja laughing their heads off. It was all about me and the woman. How did it go? Mayanja asked.

Fine. We just rode around the Slums.

What did she want?

A tour around. She wanted to see the life of the mothers in the Slums.

She must be mad. What for? asked Jabbir.

I didn't ask her, I said.

Who does she belong to? asked Mayanja.

Same answer to that too. I didn't ask, I said.

She is a dish, said Mayanja.

So you had a ride in a minister's car? commented Jabbir.

Well, I sat in his place with his wife, I said.

You might one day be a minister, who knows? All these ministers once belonged here. That DC used to live along Nandi Street, said Hussein.

But try telling them that now. You will see what they will do to you. The next day you will be behind bars, said Jabbir.

That is the whole trouble with us blacks. We don't like facts, said Mayanja. Today a poor man, the next day a king, and then you don't want to hear about it.

Yeah, that is the rule of the blacks. If you tell one of them, man,

67

we used to be together in the Slums when we were plumbers, but now you are a top guy, how about something for remembrance? he will spit in your face, I said.

What else did she want? Mayanja asked.

To know all about us, I said.

Like? asked Jabbir.

If you are learned, I said.

She is a shit. What is that to her? What concern does she have with it? said Mayanja.

We will soon find out. And then after all that she handed me this. I held out the note. A tip.

A sugar mama, that one, uttered Hussein, who seemed to be out of temper.

Yeah, that one. After all, a minister's wife. They have bundles of easy-earned corrupt money, remarked Mayanja.

Yeah. The poor common man's tax. Let them enjoy it for now. One day . . . said Jabbir and so we finished with the subject, his sentence hanging in the air.

It was nearing seven when we stored our kit away. We headed for a butchery. Tonight we thought of roasting meat. That was to celebrate the woman's money. We left it cooking and headed towards this Muchohi's Club. We absorbed one each. We took a stroll around, the main aim being that tonight we wanted to lay the bamzis. So it was to find out the recent comers.

Next day we were sitting on this skeleton of a Renault feeling worn out – we had puffed from Rori's, a pound each from those mamas – when Brazze joined us. *Asalaam aleikoum*, he greeted us.

Aleikoum salaam, we roared back.

So? he asked.

Just resting, we answered.

Last night was terrible, he said.

Why? we asked.

Cham. Took a lot of cham, he said.

Eeh? we remarked.

Man, it was terrible. We started at Charia's, then to Mama

Atieno. From there to Njoki's and ended at Machwara. There Odongo, Walker, Bez and Obadiah hijacked Susy, Rashada and Kombi. They took them to Rendezvous, he explained.

Mizoga na viruka njia, commented Hussein. Women with short futures. *Mizoga zetu za mitaani*, I added. Then the rest joined us. We all talked of last night. That is our uhuru, commented Burma. *Uhuru wa maskini*. What can we do when the whole world is leading to its end? asked Brazze. We talked of this and that and at last decided to attend a movie in the afternoon. Which theatre? asked Hussein.

Kenya, I said.

No. Odeon, proposed Brazze. It is cheaper.

No. I don't like those theatres. This Casino, Odeon and Cameo, said Burma.

Why? asked Brazze.

People sleep in them. They see the movie twice and then sleep, farting as if they were in their own houses. Kenya and Twentieth are okay. Just tip the gateman and everything is simple. You sit anywhere inside, explained Burma.

How? asked Brazze.

Just three bob. Wink at them and it will be done. But not at the end of the month when a new film is showing. By then it is always house full. You might sit on someone's seat and that might cause a mess, Burma went on.

Eh? Brazze was suprised.

You are sleeping. You don't know about that? challenged Hussein.

First time I have heard about it, said Brazze.

Not your mistake. What would a slummer be in town for? A guy like Massopo stays six months without stepping into town, joked Burma.

What would we be looking for? We have our local theatres here. We have Ukumbusho and Memorial, what would we want in town? We have tailors, markets with everything in them, clothes, shoes and everything. What else do we need? Music is here too. Hi-Fivers perform once every week. In fact, in the whole of Nairobi there is no location like the Slums. In the Slums we have everything. It is the most independent city in Nairobi, said Jabbir.

Yeah. That is Majengo, agreed Burma.

In the afternoon we went to the movie at the Kenya.

From the Kenya, the night still young, we decided to stroll around. We took to Exotica. With our cheeks bulging, we looked strange and silly. All the eyes turned around to us. We looked like intruders. Rough. Then I saw them. Two of my former schoolmates in Highway, John and Guard. They were in a corner slowly sipping coffee. I felt like pissing so I excused myself from the boys and headed to the toilet. In there a silly-looking bloodied Modess looked at me. Some women are careless. A thing like this needs care. It is too private. I came back and joined the schoolmates.

Hi, men, I said.

Ooh, Eddy. How are you, man? asked both of them.

Not bad, I said.

It is a long time since we saw each other.

Yeah, men. So, how are you pushing on? I asked.

Ooh, not bad, said John.

John, you are growing bald. I think you are feeling okay at the Community, eh?

Rubbish, man. Some nuts there are trying to undermine me, he complained.

What do you mean? I asked.

Some old fools there are trying to report me every day to my boss, he said.

That is nothing, man. Tell your brother-in-law. He fixed you, I said.

I wish you worked there, he complained.

Why? I asked.

You wouldn't have said that, he replied.

Drop dead. Your sister is a secretary to the DCA.

Then Guard laughed. What is it? I asked him.

I'm just watching the bulging on your cheeks. You are really a slummer, he explained.

70

Yeah, man. What else can I do? Just poor me, what can I do? How is Jogoo? I asked him.

Well, not bad. Just dealing with the pensioners, he answered.

Haven't you got wives? I asked.

What for? asked John.

Well you are all right, aren't you? I said.

What are women for? There is no hurry for that, said John.

Be careful not to be like Banda, I joked.

What do you mean? asked Guard.

This is what I mean. Banda took a long time. Now he says that the women of his age are grannies. That they are all worn out.

It is up to the women. They better be careful not to wear out too fast, said Guard.

Women are like flowers. They have short times for their lives. When the water is finished . . . dead. I wish you could see those at the Slums, I said.

How are they? asked Guard.

Worn out. Completely worn out. You see, there, sex is a plaything. All the young girls play it. You can never call any mtoto. She might challenge you, I explained.

Goodness me, remarked Guard. I wish I lived there.

What would you do? I asked.

Fuck them out, he replied.

You are talking shit, I said.

Why? he asked.

Utachoka. Mazee utachoka. You would be tired, man.

My God, he remarked.

Come if you want to try. You'll get all the love styles, I said.

When do you want me to come, because I feel like trying out those waziba? asked Guard.

Come any time. I'm always there. At Katanga Base, I said.

I hear that those women cry when you screw them.

Well, that you will find out yourself, I said.

How about Tuesday? he asked.

I will be there, I said.

John, you will take me, eh? He nudged Ngare.

71

I want the Muslims. How about a Mswahili? I hear they know love, said Ngare.

WaSwahili are shits. Wanafiki, I said.

Why? he asked.

It is not like you think. I wish you had lived there among them. You would hate them. Their way of life is too corrupted, I said.

Tell me.

Ah, forget it. By the way, how are the others? Sylus, Mike, Lucas, Owino and the rest of them? I asked.

We don't meet much, but they are in town here. Sylus is gone to poultry, Mike recently joined the Attorney's chamber, Lucas is the luckiest of all. You remember just after school he went to Bombay to do a diploma in agriculture? John explained.

Yeah.

I think he is back. Lucky for him, said Guard.

Yeah. His brother-in-law is a minister. Owino is a conductor with the Bus Co., said John.

I met Erick and Kelly some time back, I said.

Yeah. They have started a shoe-shining business. You can always see them there at Blu-Kat. That is their place. Washington is roasting maize at Nairobi South, said John.

Too good and too bad for them, I said. Life is tough.

Well, have you seen that lady we were at school with? asked Ngare.

Which one? I asked.

The one who was very thin.

That thin-skinned bent-foot dry woman? I said.

That's the one. That Jemmy, said John.

No. What of her? I asked.

She has been asking a lot about your whereabouts, they explained.

Why? I asked.

We don't know. Whenever we meet she has to ask about you, said Guard.

She can drop dead. Next time she asks tell her to stick her finger into her arse and leave it there. Tell her I have no money. I got no money, no job. She better take her troubles somewhere else.

72

I wonder what is wrong with the ladies? Nearly all of them are mothers with no husbands, said Guard.

It is up to them. That is their liberation. And with that I joined my gang and we left for the Slums.

In the Slums there was a show in the Memorial by the Black Golden Slummers. We went there to kill more time. Together with them were the Majutos, Mzee Pembe and Co. The hall was full. Much laughter. These comedians were terrific. Very good entertainers. We watched it. The play. Kadugunye handed me a note.

Who from? I asked.

That woman who was here. The Benz woman.

Oooh. Thank you. I took it to the light and read it. It ran:

Eddy,

I hope you are all right since last time I left you. I was around looking for you but didn't find you. I heard that you had gone to a movie.

Well what I would like to tell you is that tomorrow you are wanted at Railways HQ. I talked to one of the executives there. He told me that you should report there at 8.30 in the morning. It is room number 159. He will be expecting you. Take your certificate with you.

Try and go. I hope to see you on Saturday.

Yours,
Zakia.

After finishing it I handed it to Hussein to read also. He went through it. Well? I asked him.

Go and try, he said. You might succeed.

I wonder, I said.

Go tomorrow, he suggested. You never know.

I will, I said.

It was 8.15 by this big-eyed clock on the wall. I saw officers entering their offices. One glanced at me and made a face. I was smart. One look at me and you wouldn't need a second guess. I was a Lami man. A tarmac nut. The sun was not strong enough to fight the cold away. I was feeling cold. I took a bath in that toilet at the hall. We were four in that bathroom. It has no door. The iron doors of the toilet are all rusted. We piled our rags on this glassless window keeping our eyes on them. No joke. You might leave the bathroom naked. There are those with itchy fingers. We had no privacy. If you want privacy you can build your own bathroom. It was 8.25 when I took the lift to the second floor. I roamed the corridor looking for this door. It was on the third floor. I roamed about when I had found it, to give myself more time. At exactly 8.30 I knocked on this wood. I knocked again. Come in, a soft voice answered. I pushed it back to make a way for myself. In front of me was this silly-looking Gor woman. On her head was an oversized dead man's collection of hair. A black wig. She looked silly. I wondered how her man loved her. Perhaps her man was blind. I wondered how she came to be in this office. She was one of the right people in the wrong places. She was OK to be in the city mortuary. She would be good at sticking that cotton into the corpses. She had the eyes of a tart who at first sight would tell you how much you had in your pocket. You can see them in town. They are cool. Never in a hurry to get a mate. Not like those at Starlight and other night clubs who grab you when you pass. They have no manners. I think they never accompanied their mothers on the way to markets. They never held hands. These thoughts ran through my mind.

Morning, madam, I said.

Morning. What can I do for you?

Well I'm Eddy. Eddy Chura. I think Mr Anam is expecting me.

Well I don't know, let me check. She picked the connection and pressed a knob. A white man must be up to date with his inventions. I wondered when we blacks will invent anything. Some nut tried a plane and failed. He got no aid from the government to help him out. Some nuts could never agree to that. Jealousy. That is the trouble with us blacks. Jealous. We are born with it and we shall die with it. Very unfortunate. She talked and cut the connection. Well, follow me. Like a German shepherd I followed her tail, wriggling in these tights of hers.

She pushed this mahogany of Timsales. She let me pass. The door was shut behind me. I faced this nut. Morning, sir, I said.

Morning. What can I do for you? he asked.

I'm from Lady Zakia, I said.

Which Zakia? he asked.

God. How can I explain her? I thought. That lady whom you were with. She told me that I was expected here, I explained.

Well, I got it. Have a seat. He offered me a chair.

Thank you. I sat.

You are a Luo? he asked straight.

Yes, sir, I said.

From? he asked.

Yimbo, I said.

Yimbo makany? Which part of Yimbo? he asked.

Ramogi, I said.

I wuod ng'a? Whose son are you? he asked.

Opondo, I said.

Mer? Your mother? he asked.

Anyango, I replied.

And where are they? he asked.

Dead, I said.

And where do you live? he asked.

In the Slums. Majengo, I said seriously.

Majengo? he was astonished.

Yes, sir, I said.

And how did you meet that lady? he asked.

In the Slums there, I explained.

How? he asked, surprised.

She brought her car there for washing, I said.

Do you mean to tell that you wash cars there with waSwahili?

Yes, sir, I said.

Now what job do you want? he asked.

Anything, I said. What else could I say?

What experience do you have? he asked.

I don't have any. I have not worked before.

Then how do you expect to work in an office? He was rude.

I will try and learn, I said.

75

We don't teach people here. You are not fit to work here. How far did you learn? he asked.

Up to Form Four, I said.

What grade? he asked.

A certificate, I said. He did not ask to see it.

Well. I would very much like to help you, but not in our office here. Would you like to work in the field? I mean out from the office?

Yes, sir, I said.

How about working there at Makongeni? he proposed.

Not bad, I said.

I think they need a person there and if you would be interested in the job I could fix it up you.

I am sir, I said.

Well, they need a trench cleaner. *Chura wa mtaro*. Do you like it?

God, I uttered, without thinking. That killed me.

What is 'God' for? he asked.

No, I said, shaking my head.

You don't like it? he got up.

No, I don't, I said.

You wouldn't do it for long. We would put you on to something else after some time, when a vacancy arises in here, he explained.

No. I better wash cars, I said.

Okay. Get out of my office, black dog. *Guok*. Get out, he roared. *Guok*. Man, this nut can shout, I thought. And don't come back again. I stood my ground. If he came near me, I thought, I would punch him. I'm not a dog. Okay, I said. Can I tell you something?

What? he demanded.

Tell your secretary she has a leakage. And with that I left. Along the corridors I met with curious eyes looking at me. They closed the doors. I walked away.

I passed this Development building looking at the school leavers moving up and down. Men: you will climb that house. We climbed

76

it and got bored. They are all the same. This one and that one there, Labour, I thought. At Deacons I met this ex-girl from during my school times, Sabina. Hello, mam, I said.

Oh. Eddy. How are you?

Fine. How is you?

Not bad. Where are you from? she asked.

Somewhere down there. In one of the offices. I pointed to the direction.

So you are running away from the office? You have escaped work? she asked.

No. Just walking. I'm on the longest leave. I'm suspended till an unknown day, I said.

Why? she asked astonished.

Because I have never been employed, I said.

Don't lie. She slapped my shoulder.

No. I'm speaking facts, I said.

I don't believe you, she said.

I'm not telling you to. You can decide for yourself whether to believe or not to, I said.

It can't be. She was doubting. Life is tough, she added.

Don't worry. How about you? I asked.

I got it with the airline people, she explained.

Sure? What are you? Flying? I asked.

No. Ground, she answered.

You are lucky. Women, you are lucky. You have the green lights, I said.

What do you mean? she asked.

Just give it and the next day you have it, I explained.

You are wrong. Some use you and some never, she said coolly. Women are being exploited badly in town, she went on.

Too bad for us all. And where are you? Still in West? I asked.

No. I'm now at YWCA. That one in Ofafa. Why don't you come there?

To do what? I shot at her.

To see me. We can chat, she said.

No need, I said.

Why? she asked.

77

I don't trust you. I have no job. Also, no car. Not even a bicycle. I can't, I said.

Not even to see me? She thumbed her chest.

Yeah. You terminated my contract, don't you remember? When you took that graduate fellow. When are you marrying? I mocked her.

We are not. She was sad now.

Why? I burst out laughing.

He dropped me, she said.

Why? A beautiful baby like you? I held her shoulders.

Well. He knows it himself, she said.

Just like I hoped. You thought you were the wisest in cheating men. I warned you but you thought I was a fool. Come back to me. Eh? I said.

Do you really mean it? she asked.

Yes. I mean it really. But I am a jobless, I said.

Where can I contact you? she asked.

Come there and you will get me. Just there in the Slums. I recently saw that man of yours there, I said.

What was he doing? she asked.

What would he be doing there? He knocked and asked for a chance, I said.

Did he get it? she asked curiously.

Definitely. There are always chances there. In those mud houses, said I.

It is up to him. He will regret it, she said.

What? I laughed.

That we parted, she said.

Don't expect that. Nowadays once your man leaves you, don't expect him back. There are too many of you, I said, noticing that she was serious.

Okay, I'm going, she said and started off.

I hope to see you. Bye, I said. Good luck, I shouted.

A nice talk, I thought. It made me forget about being a dog. *Guok*. I decided to pop into immigration and see Junior and then decided not to. Why see someone who is counting his hours while you count

78

none? Shit. I went towards the court. There the security was tight. There was that trial of the attempted coup. Those guys must be feeling good. Those cells. Those cages of cells there. Too cold. Those big thick panels of doors. That big key and that big record book. I have never seen that type of a book before. I have been down there myself too, I thought. I moved on. The whole town was talking on the subject of the coup. There a group of people. There and there. Three. Four. Suppose it had succeeded? I thought. I would have died. No. I would have had a change. These buildings would have tumbled to earth. Like that Hilton. Perhaps I would have been rich. How about the properties? How about the beautiful wives? They would have been raped to death. No. How would it have been to a local down-the-heel common man? Few would have died. From them ministers would have sprung. Those kids playing in the dust half-naked, who knows what would have come to them? Those viruka always in sandals, or barefoot. Clad in khangas. So I thought to myself. Perhaps it would have removed that nut from that office. He thinks that he won't get out from that damn cement. Be careful, guy, I cursed. There are ups and downs. Today a king. Tomorrow? God knows. Everybody seemed to be blaming this tribe. This Luo. They were the chief heads. Especially that thick-lipped ex-army, Owino. A crazy nut. He caused mutiny there during his time. Shit. Man, you are a shit. Suppose I had died? I would have been free from this hell. God. I have suffered enough. I have slept in graves and yet my days are not yet over. There at Makaburini. I have tried the church but they always lock it before my arrival. I have slept in both those clubs, Mollo and Rwathia. On those sofas. The waiters knew me, I got stopped. God. What is life if this is my life? I cursed again. And walked on. Thoughts troubled my mind.

The free food at University. Both of them. Lunch and supper. Why not? The students thought I was one of them. Kibago helped me a lot. He is one of them. The janitors. God bless you. Some guys have hearts. Shit. I blamed my sufferings on this uhuru. I was brooding when I reached these former schoolmates. Around them were tins of any colour. Of all the shoes being worn. It was Erick and Kelly.

Salaam jamaa, I said. Are you okay, men?

Salimini. Fine. Where are you lost? asked Kelly.

Down there. *Mtaani*. So? Anything good so far? I asked.

What can be good, man? It is all the same. Only the news about the coup attempt. To hell with it. What have we to lose? It is up to the rich. What has a common man like you to worry about?

Let it come. It might bring some luck, I said.

Who cares? said Erick.

Where do you come from? asked Kelly.

Just from the railways. I went there and a *maskini bepari*, poor exploiter, chased me out.

Why? asked Kelly.

I said no to his favour, I said.

What was it? asked Erick.

He wants me to sweep the Makongeni mitaro. A crazy idea, I said.

He is mad, said Kelly.

That is because I have no experience, I added.

How can one be experienced while not working? asked Erick.

I wonder, I said.

Anyhow that is our uhuru, said Kelly.

Yeah. We grabbed it before time. By the way, how are the others?

Some are still hitting the tarmac. Have you heard about Yusuf? asked Kelly.

No, I said.

Hamedi and Banta? he asked.

I hear they are fishes, I said.

Yeah. Life is tough, said Erick.

How did they enter that world? Because the last time I saw them they were selling newspapers at that roundabout on Uhuru Highway, I said.

That is where it all started. Some whites seduced them and because of being so desperate and hard up, with the world of fashion competition they had no alternative. And I hear that there is good money in that business. I don't think you would remember them now if you met them, said Kelly.

80

Why not? I asked.

Too expensive. Up-to-date fashion and bundles of money, said Erick.

And Yusuf?

Yusuf is dangerous now. He can kill you, said Erick.

That quite cool chap? I was surprised.

Yeah. That one, said Erick.

Why? I asked.

He has joined them, said Kelly.

Who? I asked.

The Panga gangs.

Don't tell me. All that quietness is gone, you mean? I said.

It is gone, said Kelly.

And how are they making out? I asked.

They are making money. Good money. Recently they made ninety-five thousand in three raids, said Erick.

That is lolly, I said.

It is, man. But too dangerous. You might lose your life any time. It is a matter of death and life.

Why do you worry so much about death? I asked.

I'm not worried. Nor is Kelly, said Erick.

Then forget about death sometimes. It is matter of living, rich or poor. All the people are doing that. I wish you had seen that movie, I said.

Which one? they asked.

French Connection. You wouldn't trust any of these bigs you see in big cars. That smuggling is too much, mind you, I said.

Sounds like the one we saw, *The Organisation*, they said.

How did you find it? I asked.

No jokes in money, they said. These big people . . .

Yeah, men. Looks like the world is soon to come to an end. Everyone is out for a quick grab. Everyone is out for a get-rich-quickly. Some are on ivories and skins. Game-skins, I mean, I said.

Some on the smuggling of money, said Kelly.

That is it. The poor local man is innocent. Only when something is about to be discovered then they fall on a poor man. The slums are their first main suspects to cover the whole thing, I said.

Too bad for the slummers, said Erick.

A customer came and we said bye, wishing each a success.

It was nearing noon when I thought of lunch or felt like it. I had some coins in my pocket and I thought of Iqbal. There is satisfying food. I headed for the place. From there I took route forty. Back at the Slums I found all as usual. Hussein took me aside. How did it go? he asked.

Shit, I said. It was all shit. The nut wanted me to go and do the Makongeni trenches simply because I have no experience of work apart from washing cars, I said.

What are you? A chura? he asked.

I wonder, I said.

Uh, forget it, he said. They better stay with their jobs.

I have done so, I said. It is not their mistakes, it is the failing of the government and politicians. They started it.

That's right. It is the fruit of uhuru, he said. I wonder how it will be in the next five more years to come.

It will be terrible, I said. Our future is hanging on a pendulum.

Don't be worried, he said. Things change. It is only a matter of time. Times changes everything. Isaac Hayes has changed.

Yeah, I said. You see, there is a saying in my language that if you keep on sleeping in the middle you will never realise that at the end it is cold.

Yeah. Let us wait and hope.

That is it, I said.

In the evening we took our supper, a full glass each of cham, and killed the stink at Masandukuni with one beer each. We had no money to buy more. We went back to the wrecks. There we found the boys happy and in a file. They stood waiting each for his turn to the car. Drunkenly we asked what it was about.

It was Mahamoud Maintain, said Mayanja. He brought her here, drugged her, and left her for the boys.

Who is she? we asked.

82

A mhindi, he said. An Asian.

Where is she from? asked Amasco.

Who knows, answered Odongo.

We asked no more.

In the morning the new stories were about the Asian Bushbaby and the coup that failed. I wish it had succeeded, said Burma, who was not in the group last night. I wish it had succeeded and we could see what would have happened to those lustful politicians.

So too do I, said Brazze. Perhaps a change would have been better than how it is now, he added.

We would have stopped running from the law every time we see the cops, said I.

They are all shit, cursed Hussein.

Their mothers' buttocks, abused we all.

What do they think we are? Who do they think they are? asked Odongo.

Their mothers', abused Burma. They will pay one day.

They will explain one day how they came to get all that they have now, said Hussein.

But men, these people are grabbing, said Yossa.

No joke, replied Brazze.

And what do we call them? asked Bez.

The lustful corrupted black politicians, said Odongo.

Yeah, we all agreed to that joke. We all laughed.

Damn them all, said I.

We denounced them all.

It was Tatu, this two-shilling tart, a bamzi, who got me from the gossiping. With her my bastard. I impregnated her when I was her bodyguard. A lousy silly good job. I was to defend her when a customer refused to pay the two bob. I would fix him. I lost two of my white piano keys to a Masai. Two teeth. The half-naked Masai hit me with a club on the kisser. After acting, the nut demanded his two bucks by force. That started it all. I wish those nuts would stop walking with those clubs in town. And my time of sleeping was at ten o'clock. That was the end of the day's business. The end of the filing in of different types of men who laid her while I stood by to wait for any trouble. I went to Tatu.

How are you? She asked.

Better. When did you come back? I asked.

Recently, she said.

How is Bukoba? I asked.

Not bad, she answered.

How is the kid? I asked, fondling her.

She is fine, she answered.

Is she the one? I mocked.

Yes, she answered.

What is her name? I asked.

Bangili. Bangili Kairora, she answered.

Not bad. Hallo, Bangili. How old is she? I joked with her.

Two years six months, she answered.

That is good. Where are you going to?

Gikomba. Sokoni. To the market, she answered.

To buy? I asked.

Bananas, she answered.

That is good. With us, we are just sitting in the sun, I said.

So? Will you come home? She demanded.

What is there? I asked.

I just want to see you, she said.

Okay, I will, I said.

She went. I looked at the young girl. I laughed inside. But I wouldn't go back. When I thought of it, I wouldn't go.

Is that the daughter? they asked me when I sat down.

Yeah, I said.

Beautiful, they said.

That hurt me. I thought of them all. Eight. I have eight bastards here in the Slums.

Yes. Eight. Four buried. Buried because the mothers were lousy, careless and cheap. The mothers were puffers. Drug addicts. Drinkers. Tarts. They were dirty. It took them weeks to have a bath. Women are loose in the Slums here, to all, old and young. A plaything. To the richest and the poorest. And it is leading many to cheap prostitution. That is, after the result. The

Baby. Only a few of the slummers are working. Most of the lovers are jobless. And so are the girls, the women. They have no money for feeding. What then can mothers do? It leads them to sleeping with old buzzards to get the money for milk, napkins and clothes. To get the money for their own clothes also. And so they get a second one. That doubles her prostitution. To seduce the old slobs they have to be drunk. They have to hang around the local bars. The Masandukuni, called that name because the crates are the seats. Boxes. The boys don't offer those. They don't offer money. They are so mean. They offer them drinks, as much as they can absorb, and then at last combine into them in the wrecks of cars or anywhere. Sometimes they take them to a friend's house where a group of six or eight share the same house. One or two beds is enough. Others sleep on the floor. The women don't mind. Provided the morning comes. Most of them don't have anything to eat for even a whole day. That is because in their homes they are poor. Poor because the mothers got kicked out because of two-timing affairs. In fact most of the families are poor. It is the parents who force their daughters to prostitution. They don't offer them enough. The daughters copy what the mothers are doing. It is not unusual to hear a mother tell her daughter *Nenda ukamtoboe*, meaning to suck. And it doesn't matter in what way she will do it. She will offer herself to you or anybody. It is not strange to hear a mother or a father tell son or daughter *Jitegemee*, meaning depend on yourself. A boy will go for stealing, a girl to prostitution. That is how life is in the Slums. I don't blame the girls. But the mothers. The hungry needy poor mothers. Divorced and widows. But also the ones with husbands. They are too corrupt. Too corrupt with the outside affairs. Men and women. That is why you will find a mixture of children in a home. Marriage is not a problem. You can marry a woman from mtaa wa Juu or mtaa wa Chini. Or across the road. A never-lasting marriage. And it is no wonder that out of ten people who are passing at your doors six are her former boyfriends. And perhaps two are part-time lovers. It is the same with all. Men too. No man can claim that his wife is trustworthy. What you are doing to a friend's wife is what is being done to your wife. When Mzee Omari is playing bao or

85

ajua and you are on to his wife, don't think that he doesn't know about it. When you are in the mosque for your prayers Mzee Omari is with your wife. Don't ask why. Your wife knows that you top Mariamu. So if you find that six of your children don't resemble two, don't panic. Investigate who the dad is, and go to his wife. That way you square the hard bitter pills. And that is why the mothers are now on to the boys. A mother with grandchildren will fall in love with a boy of twenty. A boy younger than her own sons. There is no shame. They will share the same room. With all the family. And they will call you father. But don't worry if you pass the daughter. That can do no damage. The Slums is corrupt. If you want to marry, it is quickly arranged with the Kadhis. There is no problem if you have no house, provided you are working. A room in the same plot will be offered to you. You won't cook in your house. You will eat with your in-laws. But just don't make the mistake of beating her. You will get it. That Congolese Chally knows it better. He got it. It is too corrupt, this place. True. This place is accursed. It is very evil. I wonder if all those mines will inherit the deeds of the Slums. I wonder if they will have a Nandi for a granny, a Luo for a father, a Meru for an uncle, a Luhya for brother, a Chagga for a sister. I don't know which language they will speak. I don't know which names they will have. I don't know which province they will belong to. I think Coast. Most of the slummers here go to Coast. They don't admit their tribe. No one will tell you his true tribe. God bless them that they don't inherit the deeds of this place. I heard their names. And I know them. They know me too. The names are all Islamic. May they not be sold to have a day's bread. Damn this place. May God burn it and all the people. Ministers, why don't you come for your children? Managers and directors, why leave them in suffering? Why are you afraid of being seen in daytime? Why come and park your cars at a distance in the dark? Why let them be forced out at a very early age, into prostitution, making them wear out quickly? Why let them be forced into abortion because they don't have enough support for the young ones? Who will marry mothers of two, three, four? Who will marry killers? Aborters? Who will marry Rehema, Nuru? Wangare, Abiba, Rash, Sophia, Hadija, Mariamu,

Fatuma, Nyanjau, Kangwele, Bi Hawa, Mama Ali, Rita, Maimuna, Serenge, Susy, Sera, Asha, Saumu, Wanjiko, Kichwa Rungu of Landhies, Laffu, Jacinta of the Leaning Trees, the Kipus, Amina, Rhoda, Njambi, Jemima, Mumbi, Luise, Isha, Maggie of the Leaning Trees, Temmy, Cha Night, Jane, Sikuku, Alima, Mbithe, Chakwe, Akinyi, Lizzy, Lizue, Noni, Atieno, Monica, Mwajuma, Tuma, Lily, Flo, Mayi, Florence, Fauziya, Karura, Virginia, Perisi, Njiko, Julia, Wairimo, Ruth, Mary, Farida, Waithera, Amina Toy, Njeri, Mary Clare, Batuli, Vicky and the Armstrong sisters, Fatuma Mwana, Kasa, Soul Sister, Miss Kibushi, Miss Sukusu, Miss Soul, Miss Labour Day, Miss COTU, Miss Jet Age, Miss USA, Miss World, Miss Africa, Miss Nairobi, Miss Malaya? Golda Meir, *muislamu*. Who will marry Miss Majengo? Who will marry them? These women of the world? The soldiers of Women's Liberation? Christ have mercy. But no. You are the worst. You didn't marry Maria Magdalena. You died without a wife. So why should we? Mohammed the Prophet didn't, so why should we? You satisfied your appetite on your apostles and when Judas refused you called him a traitor. You feared that he would tell the world. And so too you, Mohammed. You're all the same, Gods. Maria had the first degree adultery with God. To get Jesus. Joseph was impotent. He did not know who impregnated his wife. No. He knew. But he played the cool part. The part of an incapable. Yes, this is all shit. Bullshit. A black man has no religion. He is like a flag. He follows the wind. He has nothing. Why? Simple. Christianity to me is for the Israelis, Islam for the Arabs, Hinduism is for the Asians. How about this black thief? This nut in the darkness? Shit. Pity.

4

It was Saturday and a busy afternoon. Sweat was pouring out from all and the gatty was forgotten for some time. They were stuck in the pockets as there was no time to chew them. The customers were waiting. More were coming. I was busy on this 504 and Hussein on this Citroen when slowly behind me came to stop this Alfa Sports. Red in colour.

No doubt. It was her, Zakia. *Shkamoo*, she greeted.

Marhaba, I answered.

She sat in the car listening to some stereo music in it. The sunglasses on. When I finished I joined her. That was after the guy had complained about the charge. It was a pound. When did you raise the price? he had asked. Since everything went up. Since last year when the cost of living shot up, I told him.

So? How are you? she asked.

Not bad, I said.

Yeah. Tell me. How did it go there? She asked about the railway affair.

Bad. The nut shouted me out of his office. He called me a dog, guok, and never to step in his office again. That Anam is a fellow, I said.

Yeah. It is what I expected. You see when I talked to him about you, he wanted to know what he would get after it. When I said it was only to help he made a face. I think you know what I mean. Just how you men are. He thought and took me to be very cheap. Anyhow don't worry. I will still try hard for you, she said.

I'm not worried the least. I have been without it for the past five years and I'm still alive and well. So? Where is the big car today?

It is on a safari. The man has it. He went to Nakuru, she explained.

Oh, you must be feeling good, I said.

Why? she asked.

He is rich, I said.

Forget it. You men. These rich men . . . . Hopeless. So, what are you doing tonight? she asked.

That bombed me. Why? I asked.

Just a question, she said.

Nothing, I answered.

Do you like night-clubs? she asked.

Yeah, I said, but never do I go to them.

Which one do you like best? she asked.

I have been to many. Starlight, Hallians, Small World, Sombrero, Brilliant and others, I said.

Have you been to 1900? she asked.

No, I said.

Have you been to a disco? she asked.

No. I only hear of them and complaints that they are causing so much unemployment to musicians, but I have never attended any, I said.

I will take you there to-night, okay?

That will be hard, I said.

Why?

I will look odd. The way I am. I waved at myself.

Don't worry about that. I thought of it already. What size of shoes do you take? she asked.

Eight, I said, wondering.

What colour? she went on.

I would prefer brown, I said.

And what is the size of your waist? she asked.

Last time I bought a pair of trousers, it was twenty-eight. I don't know if I have increased in size, I said, patting my waist.

And how about shirts?

I think medium, I said.

Okay. I will see you at eight. Where shall I meet you? she asked.

I think I will wait for you at that signpost ever there. Meru Street.

Okay, see you then.

I got out and she drove away, roaring the engine.

That left some talk about her.

Asked Burma: What does she want?

I said, We go to a club.

Her mother, he abused. Suck her.

And that is what they all asked me to do. To play sucker.

Isn't she a minister's wife? asked Burma.

Yeah, I said.

Her mother. That one is for suck. Their men are sucking us alive, cursed Burma. They all wished that it was them.

It was fifteen minutes past eight when I was vexed at having gone there and missed my fun with the boys by waiting for her, and she was late and the cham that I took was fading from my veins, and I was cursing her plus her husband plus her night club, her idea and my shoes and everything about her when she rolled her Alfa to a stop just near my feet on the pavement. I called her an odd name and wished she had heard it.

Sorry for being late, she apologised.

You are not late, I said. In fact I have just come here now. Not even five minutes, I lied. Which man doesn't lie, when at last the date turns up.

Then it is all right. Come on in. Where will you try them on? And she indicated the wrappings on the back seat.

That is no problem, I said. Let's park there at the hall.

We parked. I took them and told her to wait for me there. I ran to Katanga Base. I unwrapped them and found one pair of crimplene trousers, a couple of shirts, wet-look, a pair of shoes with two pairs of socks in them, a belt, a set of underwear. Shit, I called her. How did she know that I didn't have any underwear? A tie, and then a jacket. God. This woman meant it. A shopping. I changed into them leaving an item of one behind. The rest, after looking around first I lifted the seat and hid them underneath. God. If someone slept here he would find them. But where could

90

I take them? Ocham, the Dhobi, was not there. I would have left them with him only to wear them on such occasions. Man, I wished one of the boys had seen me. He wouldn't believe his eyes. I was smart like a Luo, that Luo who gets the luck to have one pair of everything. The jobless Luo. The shoes. They had that knockout punch.

That punch which floored Floyd from Liston. The same punch which made Cooper hit air when his eye got blasted by that sharp-lipped false Muslim Clay. The punch that Clay got from that butcher-man Joe. The punch that floored him from Foreman.

In them I went back to her. She was standing out of the car. Leaning on it. She was in a mini. Red.

A gold chain was on her around her neck. Rounded earrings dancing on her ears. No stockings. I just didn't know why she wore those slacks. She had the legs of a Caribbean woman. Or Hawaiian. Plump legs. Around her ankle, the left one, another small glittering gold chain, man. I think it was the first time I saw such a thing, apart from those of the banyans, being tortured by two-inch-high heels.

Ooooh. You look smart, she said. Very smart.

Do I?

Yeah. Very, she added.

Thank you. Can we go? I said.

Get in. She opened the door for me. I got in.

On the way Zakia handed me two hundred shillings. Two red notes of a hundred each. And told me that I was now the boss. We took the Government Road and turned left passing this Camay Club. Have you been there too? she asked.

Yeah. During the boogy, I said.

Then she pointed to some young girls grabbing a white passer-by. See?

Yeah, I said.

Don't you think they are young for the business? she asked.

Well, nowadays there are no young girls. The young ones are the newly born, I said.

But these are not even fifteen yet, she said.

Yeah. But their actions are over thirty, I answered.

91

What do you mean? She glanced at me and then ahead.

The men they sleep with. They are over thirty. Like that one now. I wish you could see those of the Slums. You wouldn't believe it if I tell you that they have two children or three.

Do you mean it? She was astonished.

Of course, yeah, I said.

But I can believe you. How is that place really? she asked.

Corrupted. That place is too damn corrupted. All. Young and old, I said.

Tell me, she laughed.

That is it. The place has all type of people. Richest and poorest. And perhaps the most people, I said.

Sure? she asked.

Yeah. Apart from Mathare Valley, I said.

And tell me, what is the effect of this drug, miraa? Because I have seen so many chewing it.

It is just like the dope. Good for killing time.

And does it have any effect? Does it add some power, as people claim?

No. To me no, I said.

Why? she asked.

Because I have chewed it.

Have you? she asked.

Yeah.

But I heard rumours that it adds more stimulation, she said.

Never. To me never.

We drove on. Then I asked her: Tell me.

What?

Why do you wear slacks? I mean these bell-bottoms and so on?

Fashion. It is all fashion, she defended herself.

So I thought wrong, I said.

What did you think? she asked.

I thought that women are nowadays tired of being what they are, I said.

Then if so, how about the men who play the women's role? The

92

homos? I think they are tired of being men. They want to find out what women feel. It is so strange, she said.

Julius Caesar did it and so did that great artist Da Vinci, I said seriously.

That is it. You are the worst, she said.

I hope they get pregnant on their backs, I said. We drove on in silence.

At the club, from one hundred-shilling note, I got eighty back. Inside we couldn't move. The light was very dim. We stood at the entrance to focus. Having adjusted ourselves, we moved to a table. Then ordered a double vodka and a bitter lemon. I took a double whisky, dry. We repeated the order and got on the floor at a new release of JB, a Popcorn feeling. We danced. From Popcorn we got into a soul, then a Congolese rumba. From that into a Cha Cha. Then came the blues. That brought us into contact. Body contact. Man, what a smooth thing. We swung coolly. So disco was not after all bad. I wanted to see it. When we broke we carried our glasses around. That was my idea. They are here too, the glass-pickers. Or bottles. We came to the machine. She told me that her husband wanted to buy one too. But that she refused. We took a keen look at this machine. A record-player, tape, amplifier and connected speakers. An operator behind it. Watching more of it I felt a touch on my buttocks. I pretended not to feel it. It continued. I turned to see what the hell it was about.

Turning around I saw this white man looking at me. He must have boozed a lot. He was drunk. In his hand a glass gripped tight. Whisky in it.

Hello, I said.

Hello. What a wonderful night, he said.

We looked at him. Who the hell is he? we wondered. Then . . . Where is your table? he asked.

The lady fired back at him. We don't have one. Ours are at home.

That made him realise that I was not alone. He apologised to her. Have a round on me, he offered.

No. Thank you, she answered him. He bowed and disappeared

in the audience. Silly white, remarked the woman. They think that every one is on that game.

What game? I asked.

The man-woman game. Homosexuality, she fired.

God. What made him think of me in that game? I asked.

I wonder, she said, her arm around my shoulders.

I wish we had given him more chance to go ahead. He would have stopped from today, I said. With that we dug the music. She then left me for their Labour Ward marked 'Ladies'. I went for ours. Smiled at my silly self in this mirror on the wall. I winked at my own face. With the third order we moved around swinging happily. Then we came to meet them. Hemedi and Banta. I still could make them out in this club. Well, they are okay, I thought, just as I was told about them. Damn expensive. We approached them drunkenly. Hello, men, I said.

At first they couldn't recognise me. Then it was Banta. Oooh Eddy, how are you man? He offered a hand.

Fine and beautiful, I said, shaking his hand.

And is this the wife? asked Hemedi. We heard that you got married.

Yeah, I'm the wife, she answered them. Any wonder? She was drunk.

No wonder, answered Hemedi, apologising.

She is Zakky, I said. And this is Banta and his friend Hemedi. I'm what you can call a Casanova. We laughed at that. So, how is life?

We are just pushing on fine, they answered. How about you?

Just as you see me. I moved my hand over my stomach.

Place of work? asked Hemedi.

No work. Just a loose playboy. And you? I asked.

We are with this airline firm, said Hemedi.

Which one? Sabena, EAA, BOAC or which? I asked.

BOAC, said Hemedi proudly.

As what? I asked.

Flying stewards, said Hemedi. Banta was uneasy.

That is good, men, I said. So you have flown to all European countries? Yeah. Those places have life. No joke. Not like ours here. He grinned.

When did you join them? I asked.

Now almost two years. By the end of this month we will be on leave, he said.

And where will you go for your holidays? I asked.

Not yet decided. You see they have these staff tickets. We might go to London, he said. Banta had moved to a friend.

That is sure good. With us we are still fooling around here. And with that we parted. Having wished each other nice times. All crap, I told her. Those are all lies.

Why? she asked.

They are homos, I said.

How do you know? she asked.

There is no secret to that. They are my former schoolmates. They were on this newspaper-selling before they turned to this game, I said.

Well, it is life in the city, she said. Developed big cities.

That is it. The damn high life, I said. We danced.

We left at two, passing Hemedi and Banta in the company of two whites. A Singh and one who looked like the man we had met at the disco. Do you believe me? What I told you? I asked drunkenly. I do. We drove away in silence.

We came to a stop at this petrol station opposite Brilliant Club. We parked the car, locking all the windows. We tipped the petrol attendants. Drunkenly we walked to the club holding each other for support. We paid six shillings. In there we danced no more. We went up the stairs and booked a room.

In the morning, we took a bath and drove to Panorama Café for a breakfast. Taking a shoe-polish, we drove back to the Slums. She dropped me and had her car washed while we stood and chatted. I noticed that the boys had some talk about us. Finished, she drove off, promising to come back. I went to check what I had left last night. Nobody had disturbed them. I picked them up and joined the boys. The topic was, how was last night? I told them all about it. They admired the clothes. They congratulated me for playing sucker. I took my clothes to Ocham's laundry. There they would be safe. I would leave them there and only wear them on my state occasions. I went back and did nothing. I had money in my pocket. The balance of last night.

At lunchtime, we took to Riatha Hotel. We took full biriani each. Then passed through Sophy and bought our afternoon killer, mairungi. I didn't feel like chewing it. Instead, with the boys chewing, I sipped coke. I was very lazy. We talked. I told them how silly I looked at the Café. I couldn't tell anything from that menu. I knew none of the food on it. That caused laughter. How can poor maskini like us know about menus? asked Burma. Rich men's places, our rags are not wanted there. We are used to buying the thirty-cent oil and carrying it with us to 'Kwa Mama Kiosk', how can we know about menus? remarked Abbas. Those people have no manners even, commented Jabbir. Instead of staying in their town bars you will see them in our Masandukuni with us. Especially in that councillor's bar. The former office of DP, Democratic Party.

But how did that building turn into a bar? asked Suleiman.

Who knows? They are the power, said Yossa. They are the Government.

But that guy is a nut, said Juma. If you want a house in the city, you must go and see him, drink in his bar and then tell him your troubles.

Just like the Mafia, added Bez. That is Mafia style.

That is it, agreed all.

Not only him but all of them. The ministers too. They are all gangsters operating on the common man, said Urai.

It is an open exploitation, said I. They regard us as churas. The down-at-heel maskini. They want us to kneel before them and adore them.

That is what they better forget, said Burma. One day we shall overcome and they will feel the bitter part of it. They will repent how they ran from the Slums, forgetting that they came from there. They will know the importance of the Slums. They will know that in the Slums great people are still there.

The boxers will still come from there, said Abbasi, pointing to Steve, a Slummer who had been to Mexico in the Olympics. We don't produce them in Lavington or Muthaiga or those places they pretend to be staying in.

Asalaam aleikoum, greeted Steve.

Aleikoum salaam, we roared back.

Yeah, man, begun Burma. Tell us about that tequila. Is it like our cham?

That is terrible. That stuff is no joke. Too strong. Olulu drank a full bottle and slept for three days without waking. We thought he was dead, said Steve.

That is why the Sombreros are proud of it, said Suleiman.

Why did you go there and get knocked out in the first round? asked Yossa.

There are tough boxers out there, man, he defended himself.

So when you got knocked out you took their women, eh? remarked Hussein.

What else? We got into drinking and their women. How else can we remember the games and places? he asked.

There is no other way, man, said Burma. Just enjoy and buy the fashions. It is the Government's money, he added.

Not their money, corrected I. The common man's sweat.

But Phillip did it, said Steve. That nut boxed. They favoured his winning.

He got red carpet treatment in London, said Suleiman.

The Slums are important, said Yossa. We have every type of people. Boxers, politicians, broadcasters, writers and all.

Forget about the politicians, said Burma. One day they will tell the common man how they came to possess the riches they came to have.

We stopped talking when these two Datsun cars rolled in to a stop. We knew them. They were Special Branch. Our daily visitors here whenever a robbery had been done in town. We watched them moving from car to car, from taxi to taxi. We looked around to see if he was in. He was not around. Too bad for the corrupted feet. Bilali was not in. His 404 was not around. After failing to see him they drove away. Too bad for the Slums.

Whenever a raid has been done it is always the Slums first. Not the Kitsuru or Muthaiga, said Burma.

To hell with them, said Suleiman. Sometimes they are only after a tip.

Yeah, agreed Mayanja. When they are flat broke.

When broke they look for a gang leader, I said.

And what is wrong with that? asked Juma. Even if it were me I would take the tip. Corruption is everywhere. Take the example of that Martin, that inspector and his friend Masharubu. They are horrible.

Martin most, said Yossa. He is only after women. If he sees a good girl new to him, he must chase her. He will pick up any boy and beat him up to scare him. Afterwards he will tell you to seduce that girl for him. Even if she is your girl. If you refuse, too bad for you. A false charge will be on you.

Masharubu is only after money. He is always after busaa women, said Suleiman. One day they will be beaten up. Because of being in plain clothes. It will be like Mathare.

That day nobody will sleep. GSU will have free women. They will rape them like hell, said Bez.

Still on our talk, came this long blue American Pontiac. In it four occupants. Kipanga was the driver. A funny chap. This comedian. His head quite hairless. Very clean shaved. They were all on miraa. We switched our attention to them. Mostly Kipanga. We talked of his career as a comedian. That was his talent. A natural talent. We talked of how he talked in the different accents of different tribal tongues. He is a funny man. You couldn't fight him. He would make you laugh and forget your quarrel with him. He would give logic and make you look a fool. Perhaps guys like Mark Forest Sammy would fight him. The characters who understand no logic. They bought some gabba and drove off. We laughed at his Pontiac which had no back windscreen. We wondered about him. Not bad, we said. He is one of the Slummers who live through guts. In the Slums life depends on your guts. That is how we are. Our lives depend on our guts.

In the evening after our supper, we took to our quick gulps. Then to Masandukuni. There we found Susy, Rita, Luise, Rash, Fatuma, Amina, Adija, Ruth, Nuru, Abiba, Mariamu, Wangare and Sera. All mothers and aborters. They were now out for

98

hunting. Hunting the slobs' drinks. And it is not their mistake. For I thought they were forced to it by the poor life in the homes. I pitied them because of that. They were here for that and they all knew that. And so she won't refuse your offer. Take her home or to an alley and give her, her due. What a misfortune. A misfortune to the beautiful would-be good wives. Perhaps this place should be demolished. It is a lost city. Losing the lives of so many. Me, included. But where would I go? Along the River Roads on the pavements you can't sleep. That is, unless you are one of them. And of the same tribe. There is tribalism. Too bad. Too bad a mistake was done in the death of this economy guy, this T.J. It is a part of and the main cause of the falling apart of things. It was a mistake and a mistake that is still regretted. Regretted because he was supposed to come to the Slums and explain to the slummers about the programme of the New Pumwani estate. He had been approached by the slummers on the proposition concerning the rents. He had fought for them and wanted the rent for the houses to be not over seventy shillings for all the three rooms. That was because they were built for the sake of the slummers and slummers only. That was because it was and still is hard for the slummers to pay a rent of more than twenty shillings a month. He was supposed to come on Sunday to give us the result. He came on Friday from Ethiopia and got the bullets in his chest on Saturday afternoon. He died along with everything for the Slums. The rent of the new houses went up to four hundred and fifty a month. If a slummer can't afford to pay a rent of twenty-six shillings a month, how will he pay four hundred? The houses were not meant for them. Too bad for you, great son and true son of Africa and the world. No one's death will compare with yours. Rest your head in Heaven.

We ordered our drinks and sipped them slowly, watching the people around. We watched Rashada being taken away by this old Mkamba. And so was Susy and Abiba. Too bad, ladies, I said.

What did you say? asked Hussein.

I said too bad.

Too bad for what? he asked.

Don't you see them? The way they are being taken by old slobs?
I asked.

Well, what can they do? They are looking for a living, he said.

It is okay. Everyone wants to live, I said.

From the stores we made our way back to the wrecks. At Kabete's Shujaa Tailors, we came to a stop. It was because of this red light in the middle of the road. Along the pavement lined the watchers. We played nosy to see what it was. Ah. Shit. It was the road-block police checking on cars. We crossed and entered our wrecks. But instead of sleeping we talked about our childhood deeds. Hussein? I called.

Yeah?

Did you ever go to Buru Buru? I asked.

To do what? he asked.

Did you ever go hunting in those sisals near that bridge? Dandora?

I went there only once. A snake nearly bit me. I used to go to Mkuru. How about you? he asked.

I did. Also I went to Mkuru. Did you eat those dustbin crumbs? I asked.

Which ones? he asked.

Mangima, I said.

Yeah.

And did you pull yourself along on tufts of grass to clean your shit?

Who didn't do that? Perhaps the boys of today. They don't even use the cobs. We laughed.

There is no life nowadays like the past times. It is even hard to urinate nowadays because of the City askaris. If you try, they will tell you finish and we go. They won't even let you fly up, I said.

It is time. Times move. They won't allow you to shake off the drops, he said.

I wish they would come back, I said.

Sorry for your wishing. They won't come back, he said.

Tell me, I said.

What? he asked.

Why do women compete with us in wearing pants?

I think they want to turn themselves into us. They are tired of being what they are, he said.

But that won't stop us recognising that they are women. They will always bend when shitting or pissing, I said.

That is it, he agreed.

And do you know that soon women will start paying dowries to marry us? I asked.

They have started that already. They don't wait nowadays for boys to approach them, he said.

I think soon we will be having forced marriages. Otherwise the women will start raping us. Men are not interested in marriage. They marry and wed for only a night. The next day the woman is gone, I said.

We are lucky that we were born male, he signed.

Yes man, nobody to bullshit you, I said.

It is all shit, we agreed. With that we rolled into the land of dreams.

It was Monday afternoon when this double RR rolled to a stop. We watched this car. This Rolls Royce of the British CD. It was not for washing. In it was my friend Johnson Gichuru. We formed a friendship when in detention. That was after we had been got for trespassing there behind the Shell BP on the rails. In the detention we were put in the kitchen. There he told me how he obtained his licence. He took driving lessons at Eastleigh where now the New California stands. When he had had enough lessons at fifty cents a round, he went for a test. He failed. He went again and failed. In all he failed three times. At last he was given an idea. A short cut to it. He passed through the back door. Paid two hundred and the next day he had the licence in his pocket. He had come now for the dope. I went and said hello to him. Hi, Johnson?

Ohh. Hello mister, how are you? he asked.

Fine, man. So how is it?

Not bad. Just pushing on fine. I got into the car.

So, still not yet? he asked.

Not yet, man. Our days are not yet. They are coming nearer every day, I said.

Yeah, he agreed.

101

So your hippies are still on the dope? I asked.

They are still on it. They can't leave it, after all it is very cheap here, they say. Not only them but also the very important people are on it. They are puffing it like hell, he said.

And you are still making profit out of it? I asked.

Why not? I have to. They are fools and so I have to. Whenever they ask for it I increase the price. They have money and so no argument, he said.

After all, free transport is supplied and no one to suspect it, I said.

Who can suspect me with the Queen's flag dancing on the bonnet? he asked.

Nobody, I agreed.

And where is this Roris? he asked.

I don't know, but I think he must be around. I called out to Safi.

Yeah, he answered.

The stuff, I said.

No stock, try Kadugunye, he said.

I called for Kadugunye. He came and took the order. He brought thirty rolls. Johnson took them, paid and tipped me a five. With that he rolled the car away soundlessly. The taxi man envied it. The car was more than a house. Then an unexpected downpour of rain started. Too bad. We hated rain. It washed the cars while moving and so they were not brought here. Very few came. It stopped in the evening, and though we waited no car came. Only the curses of the quickers came. Jumped and fell into the water mixed with shits. Men have troubles, I thought. We watched these hungry folks out for a kill. In the evening we left for Rash's kiosk. From there we took to Mama Atieno's for the vyang. From there feeling not much like walking I thought of seeing Wamboi and decided against it. Instead we entered the Billiard and Snooker room. Coming out I looked and near this Pontiac stood Grace, Sammy's sister. Shit, I cursed her. What does she want?

Go and ask her, replied Hussein. It is cold, you might get a heater.

Perhaps. I went to her wondering if perhaps she wanted me to

102

accompany her to boogy. It is a long time since that day we danced there at Camay. That day she was very much afraid of those gangs. The Sun Valleys, Sicheki and that one of Hilton from Eastleigh. They were hijackers of dames. Hijacking them and combining into them. Eight, nine or even ten boys. Hello, I said.

Hello. Where is Sammy? she asked.

He was around. I think he is just around some place, I said.

So what are you doing now? she asked.

Nothing. Just watching and chatting of nothing good, I said.

Or are you on a hunt? she asked.

What hunt? I asked.

Any hunt, she said.

No, I said.

And how is Camay? she asked.

I don't know. It is a long time since I was there, I said.

Is it since that day? she asked.

No. I went there three or four times more. So today are you off? I asked.

Yeah. I just came to take some things of mine from mama.

So, how is Uplands? I asked.

Boring. Too boring and worse at the weekends. Too quiet and lonesome. You want to come there? she asked.

Who can I come to? I know nobody there, I said.

Come and see me. Or won't you be allowed? she asked.

By whom? I asked.

Your Swahili women, she said.

Who are they?

Don't pretend. I know all about you here in Katanga Base, she said.

So Sammy has told you everything?

Not Sammy. After all, I don't see Sammy myself. He is never seen at home, she said.

Then who told you? I asked.

No one. Who doesn't know the Swahili habits? Hadija told me.

Which Hadija? I asked.

That of Shauri Moyo, she said.

Well then. So what? I asked.

Nothing. I want you to come there, she said.

When?

Let's say Saturday, how about it?

What time? I asked.

Afternoon, she said.

I will be around. Then I will come, okay?

Have some cash when you come, I'm always broke, she said.

I know about it. That is no worry. Bye and see you on that day, I said.

I will be around and waiting. She left. I went back to the boys.

It was Friday and the worst news came to the Slums' boys. Two of them had got picked up for a robbery. They played a kabari, robbery with violence on a policeman. Too bad for Gachui and Kachafu. The beating they got will remain in their minds to remember. We mourned. It was Saturday afternoon and the starting of the month of Ramadhan was near. The month of fasting. *Mwezi wa Toba!* The fasting was to start on Monday. So tonight and tomorrow its evils would be spoken of. Everything would be done tonight and tomorrow. That is, the lunch would be stopped. There would only be a slight mouth-wetting in the evening after mwathini had announced some prayers. The main heavy dinner or dakku was to be eaten at midnight. And that is when men and women are allowed to make love. It is a month when all the women are clad in buibui as a mark of respect for the holy month. It is a month of remembering the prophet Mohammed and Allah. A month when there is no uttering of dirty language. No admiring of women. No dirty thinking of shit. For your satisfaction, you have to wait till midnight. I wonder how many are true observers. I mean true Muslim fasters. Perhaps the old ones. Those who have seen the best part of life and the worst part of living. The ones who are every day counting the days after the morning is gone. The ones who bless the coming of the new day by folding a small finger counting the remaining days. At daybreak they would raise up their hands to the sky, praising God for letting them see the new day. The ones you will hear saying, *Ee Walla Mola ametubariki*. The ones who cry when they think of a coffin. Too bad they are never buried in a coffin. Once buried with all the soil on you, you have no chance of rising up. The ones who cry when they think of their past days. And especially men.

With this I thought of Sheikh Ambari. He was always seated at the entrance of the mosque, in a tarabushi, a kanzu, a coat on top and a bakora. This old bull must have been a good enjoyer. At the sight of a passing woman who had hips, you would see him crying. Crying because he had no more power. Sheikh Ambari was one of those who could do anything to a mama. Too bad he chose to be sitting at the mosque where they all passed on their way to bus stops or taxis, or to market. They threw their hips and buttocks at the sight of men. And that set men off to hooting and whistling. Especially Tom, Cochio, Peter, Mbithi, John, Muganda, Brown, Ali, Kulumbu and the rest. Too bad for Sheikh Ambari and his henchmen at the mosque. These old men. Hatari. Their bastard daughters and sons can be found in any corner of the Slums. Some even have their false daughters to substitute for their mothers. Like that father of Nuru. Nuru's mother is old and cold, the slob is old but an old cat who knows and still drinks milk. That is *Kama mama kama binti*. Like mother like daughter. It is a secret, but in the Slums there is never a secret. In the Slums everything is known. And that is why the politicians want it demolished because their secrets are known here. Like Old Mwangi. He is a plumber in the City Council. He hates friendship. Sometimes when drunk, he blasts the whole of his life history to us about the Slums during their time. He would start, all friends are hopeless. Most of my friends are now ministers but they have all forgotten about me. We used to drink and do all the things together, but now they are all running in big cars with big tummies and drinking whisky instead of busaa that we used to drink together in Gogo's house. That woman, we owe her money. The credit money when we drank her pombe. We worked together in the Council as plumbers. That bearded Kaggo liked very much to play this what you call karata. *Ganda Tatu*. Three Cards. We used to do a lot of things together in the Slums here, but now where are they? Perhaps they only see me in their dreams, when they dream of this place and what we did together. But the PM is good. He passes here sometimes. One of these days I will wave him down and ask him to coffee in my home. We will talk of our past times. And with that he would end his comment. He is a funny old man. Always in a tarabushi, a hammer and his tools for plumbing, and whistling. He lives in Bondeni.

While I was still brooding, Hussein poked my ribs. Hey man, what are you thinking?

Nothing, I said. Just some silly thoughts.

How much money have you?

Nothing, man, I said. Why?

We should go to a movie in town, he said. There is one that everyone is talking about.

What do they call it? I asked.

I hear that it is called *As Naked As Wind From The Sea*, he replied.

What is the story about?

A sexy film, that is all I hear.

Well, not bad, I said.

We can go and waste time there. After all, the business won't be so good anyway.

Not bad, I said. But I'm low, I complained.

That is no worry. That woman gave me some few pounds to waste.

Who? Adija?

Yeah, so why not waste them?

Your idea and I don't oppose it, I said.

Let me wash my face and then we can go.

Me too, I said. The dust of this place can kill the eyes.

Never. We would have been blind by now, he said.

Yeah, I said. I wonder how long a white man can exist in this kind of place without getting TB.

Monkeys they are, he said. We laughed.

From the tap we moved to the bus stop under the hot sun. Behind us dust blew, making the boys curse. The bus took a long

106

time to come and Hussein decided that we had better take a taxi. I said it was all all right with me. We took Kulumbu's.

In town we dropped at this Prudential Building. He paid five shillings and never bothered about the change. His money, I thought. We went for the queue. It was so long that I decided to look ahead for someone I might know. I left him covering the space. The crowd looked at me with sharp eyes as if demanding to know whether I was going to get a space before them. The sun was too much for queuing. Near the ticket booth I found Walter, a friend of Burma's. It was a relief. Hello, Wally, I said from behind.

Aah, man, he said turning back to me. How are you?

Fine, man, I said.

So you too have come?

Yeah. The afternoon is long and no place to kill it, man.

And so it is with everyone, he said.

Yeah. Let me bring you the money and you do the booking for us, eh?

Who are you with? he asked.

Hussein, I said.

Where is he?

At the back, man.

Do it.

Thank you. I went for Hussein.

Let's go ahead, Walter is there, I told him.

We moved up to Walter. It is a relief, man, said Hussein. The sun is hot. We told Walter to get us two tickets for six shillings each and stood aside to wait for him. Hussein went for the juice tins and came back with three of them. When Walter joined us he took his tin and decided to sit at the bar while we in turn decided to cross towards the British High Commission to watch a scene where there was a crowd. We joined it and watched them seated on mattresses, desperate Asians in need of going to Britain. They were all claiming to be British nationals. What they all needed was an entry into Britain but they had no visas and permits to enter there. They did not even have work permits for them here. The sit-in had been in the newspapers for a long time.

107

Behind them stuck on the windows with Sellotape were placards covered with writing. They claimed to have no work permits. That they were waiting for visas to enter Britain. We watched them. They looked quite helpless. Just like rats in a cage. With sorrowful eyes. Eyes of helpless rats. I switched to the placards. Some had '79 days remaining' on them. One asked 'Are we second-hand citizens?' Another had 'Senior Bachelor Heath, what are you waiting for?' 'Are we not humans too?', read another. 'Is it because you are not yet married that you don't have human feelings for children?' Another read, 'Sir Alec, what do you think of our children's future?' and many more. I turned to Hussein. Did you know that Heath is a bachelor? I asked.

No, he said.

He is, I said, pointing to the placard about Heath.

And did you know that that one of Canada too is single? I asked.

Why should I bother? he answered. Their problem.

And so is that one of Libya, I went on.

What is it to me? Perhaps they are afraid of women.

No. They are mean about money. Do you know how Nixon got his name? I asked.

Which name? He eyed me.

Richard, I said.

No.

He is Rich but Hard, I said. He appeared not interested.

We looked at them. Looking at them I thought of those who got chased from Congo. At that time I was at school at St Patrick's. We used to escape lessons and go to Makadara Station to watch them. We would buy scones to give them. They had nothing. No money. Some were naked. Some half. Others had only half of a pair of pyjamas. Their children yelled because of hunger. They had nothing to eat. So we enjoyed feeding them with scones and biscuits. It was fun as we took it. All their belongings had remained back in Congo. They escaped the massacre. The Congolese wanted to rape them, eat them alive and kill them. They had sucked enough from the Congolese. That was a lesson to them. That national hero Lumumba was tough. Those whites who were the victims won't forget that man. And these looked exactly like those whites. Now they are no different from that black man of the Park, Mr Sebastian, when you feed him a banana. They will take any crumbs from a black man. They are all the same, I thought. They all forget. They shouldn't have been given shelter here. After uhuru, we should have done the same. We should have raped them and kicked them out of our land. Because one of them here blurted his mouth and called our Excellency PM a man of darkness and death. Silly guys indeed. These whites. They are lucky that our Old Man is a man of forgiveness of the past. A true statesman. Otherwise . . . Any figure apart from blacks should be kicked over the Mediterranean Sea to his motherland. They are poor there, but once in the land of a black man they take possesion of the black man's property. Out with the white pig, I found myself saying. Kick him over the sea and live alone in peace. Leave the black primitive monkey alone in his dark land. He needs no civilisation. Pack that back to your snow-white land. Out with the Arabs. They bought us like camels. Chaining a black man around the neck naked with his mother and dad, raping the mother. Out with Johnnies who stuck bottlenecks into our women at Gilgil barracks. As I was shouting all these, the crowd turned to me. Asians, Europeans and any pocketed black gorilla looked at me. Perhaps they were wondering whose cook I was, or saying look at the black monkey, perhaps he stole his master's whisky. We strolled away.

We strolled ahead towards the Law Court, leaving behind the gathered crowd. Hussein laughed his head off at what I had said about the Asians. It is too bad to grow up in a country not your mother's, I said. There comes a time when you know the importance of your own country.

Yeah, but that depends, he said. Problems are problems to all humans.

Then I pointed towards the court. See that building? I asked.

Yeah.

From there you come either dead, jailed or a free man, I said.

That I know, he said. It is where the coup men got their terms, eh?

It is, I said. I wish they had succeeded.

Why?

We wouldn't have been the same, I mean our lives, I said.

Yeah, he agreed. We would be having another type of life.

Too bad it failed, I said.

I wonder where the politicians would have run to, he said.

God bless them in the meantime, I said. Let them eat the fruits.

In the name of the Father, the Son and the Black Ghost. He did the cross from right to left.

We laughed.

We would have stopped running from the law all the time, I said.

Yeah. In fact I am tired of doing that really, that running.

And what is the time? I asked.

Two thirty, he said.

Still forty-five minutes more to go, I said. Let's walk towards the Parliament.

No, that is a long boring walk, he said.

And have you been to the Parliament? I asked.

What for? I'm not at all interested. How about you?

Yeah. A friend of mine lives there.

And who is she?

She is not a woman. He is a friend, I said.

His name?

Junior. He is a nice chap. He took me around the building and inside it.

What is it like?

A good place for marriage, I said. I mean Farouk's style.

What do you mean, Farouk's?

You just sit on the speaker's chair and watch the ball, I said.

Is that all?

No. I saw the time-keeping bottle with, I don't know, salt in it which is always turned upside down when a member is speaking, I said.

What else?

We popped in to the library, and saw the place for that PM's torch, that when it is not there there is no motion.

And what is it for?

It represents the Old Man. I mean when he is not in.

What else?

The former House, too, where we had Representatives and Senate. From there I went to the tower where that clock is. Eh, what is the time you said it was?

I said two thirty.

And how about now?

Maybe two thirty-five or more.

Look at that one on the Parliament, it says two thirty, who is right?

I don't know. Let us ask some one.

Excuse me, I said to a passer-by. What is the time, please?

Twenty minutes to three, he answered.

Thank you. I wenk back. You are correct. That damn clock is sleeping, I said. It is cheating the public. What a shame.

To whom? asked Hussein.

To whoever is concerned with it, I said. His head is sleeping too like the clock.

He said nothing. We then took Simba Street and branched on to Kimathi Street. At the statue of a dog at Deacon's I told him how it had once scared me so much when I had been into that shop that I knocked down a pregnant white woman, who knocked her hardwon fruit on the rack on her way to the ground.

It was all Noi's fault who caused it. I wanted to punch him but he was wise to me, and stood far off, laughing. He ran towards Pop-In when I approached, laughing and calling me a coward. You would think that the end of the world was near by his laughter.

Walking towards Cameo we met with a slummer, Mchina, with his mother, who perhaps life had hit even worse and turned her to begging. They looked horrible. You could never believe that this chap Mchina was once a ping-pong champion in the Slums. He had the swollen cheeks of a drunk. They were on the last stage of some slummers.

Yap mazee, he told us.

111

Yeah, we answered back. Doing it time eh? we asked.

Yeah man, he answered. His mother turned her dirty hands to Hussein for alms which Hussein gave.

Asanti mwanangu, she said. Thank you, my son. We moved on.

The last stage, we said.

That is life, said Hussein. Mchina is having all the bad part of it.

Yeah, I said. Sometimes he is seen seated in town and hiding one of his feet, shaking his hand as if a cripple, I said.

What else is there for him?

Well, that is how it is.

How about his sister? he asked.

Drinking and puffing in the Slums with the old slobs.

What a pity, he said.

On Government Road, we came upon Chhani's window. Here some couples stood. They were explaining to each other about the bullet hole in the window, the spot where this man, son of Kenya, was shot. Mr T. J.

Some guys have guts, we said. To be an assassin you got to have guts, the killing guts. We moved on. On the way we met this Ali, a slummer who had turned into a homosexual and all because of the good things of life. We cursed him. Hussein spat. With him a Boer, perhaps. I hoped he would get pregnant on the back and give birth to a creole. We then decided to take our way back. The queue was still long. We handed in our tickets and went in to the directed seats. We were all wrong. That tipping must have failed. Each seat was occupied and still more people outside were coming in.

When the news pictorial started it was all fine. But the trouble came when a funeral car appeared on the screen. The man to be buried at least looked like someone big. He was being taken to church for the last prayers and hymns. It brought again the memory of the assassination. I thought also of the last time I was in church.

The last time I was in church or near it was when this economy man, T. J., was brought in to have a requiem mass on his body.

112

That day every slummer came to attend his mass. Muslims and pagans. The rich and the beggars. Too bad for the beggars it was. They were not allowed in. They stood surrounding the church, behind the fence. Others watched from the tower of this Inter-Continental Hotel. At that time it was only a skeleton. We, the slummers, just stood on this grassland facing the church. We waited for his body to be brought from the mortuary. No one was happy. The day was dull. Mourning was everywhere. It was bad on the day he was gunned down. No one believed it. It was a shock. That day I was in boogy. At Camay. Camay was my favourite. When the news reached the corners, it was as if the end of the world had come. The first question was, who gunned him? Then it turned out sour when the facts came to be known, who was responsible. Things split from that day. Gaps formed between tribes. The unity broke. Fear started on that day. No one would trust a fellow not of his tribe. The slummers couldn't believe it, as he had promised them the new flats. So when the news spread all the town businesses came to a stop. All the boogies came to an end. Everyone had to run home, for security. If you had a wife, you wanted to die with her. Too bad for us, the car sleepers. We had nowhere to run to. So we ran from town. Pedestrians left their bikes behind. They thought they could run faster on foot. Death smelled everywhere. Every place smelled of war. It was painful. Painful because no man would fit the shoes of this boy. The boy who had no grudge against anybody. A smart, polite, charming, social man. A man of fashion. A man of the people. A born politician. An orator. That Saturday no one slept a wink. Fear gripped the heart of all. Every slummer boy had with him a weapon. An iron bar, for defence. If one slept the other took guard. At any slight noise, he would wake the other. There was no time even for the quicker.

So when the body at last came, brought by that funeral car, behind it followed a stream of others. That included the family car too. So we watched it. We watched it. We watched it being carried to the church. That added to it. The pain. The pain of a guy you used to see and the fact that you will never see him any more. That was after every stone had been turned to save him. The days in the mortuary helped not at all. So when he went in to the church no more people were allowed in. Only the VIPs. No worker was allowed in, no job-seeker. With the family, the VIPs and the dignified were the police in uniform and the plain-clothes ones. Mostly the CIDs. The down-at-heel common man was to watch from afar. We watched. Men and women. Young and old. With no one talking to his friend. The only sound was of their scratches from the disturbances of lice that they had on them. Another reason why they were not wanted inside. They might leave them on the benches. Racism in the church. The house of the so-called God. Jesus was the worst racist. He blessed only the Meirs. The Israelis. We waited. Others on the hilly side of the Park. Others on top of the Parliament tower. Perhaps Junior was one of them. He lived there. We waited. And strange enough, there was no sun torturing us. The afternoon was blue. We waited. Then at last it came. His Excellency's car. The PM. The big one of his five German gifts. With it the bodyguards. And the motorcade of police traffic. It rolled to a stop. The security men tightened the cordon. It was so tight that at a slight raise of your arm you were a goner if seen. Then the car door was opened. His Excellency got out. That started it. The cries and boos. *Dume for Medu!* They roared all over. And from all sides. They repeated it. And a third time.

Then it happened. It happened right in front of me. And it was one of the criers. He threw a shoe over to the car. The Excellency's car. The big Benz. The bullet-proof car. That started the fun. Fun as it was to me. Because we were chased and came back. Chased again from the area around the church, some towards the Law Court, some towards the Parliament, that was my group, some towards the Park, those on the skeleton of Inter-Continental Hotel came down better than monkeys because they didn't know how they came down. Death was at hand. People ran in every direction. And then they all came back, laughing. It started again. They ran, leaving behind pairs of different types of Bata products, shoes. Akalla, Tanga and all kinds. Champalis too. Slippers. In running there was no shame. Ladies pulled up their tights. Pulled them up, leaving the mountains for strip teasers to watch. Man. It was terrible. That fun went on for some time. Then more reinforcements were called in. The GSUs. Who could dare laugh going back? They formed a cordon. In a good disciplined file, with batons and tear gases. They chased the crowd away. That again added to the violence. Chased from the Cathedral, they took revenge on windows. Stone-throwing started. Anybody was a target. Cars on the road got stopped. If you didn't stop you got it. The drivers were forced to thumb. Thumbing the sign of the Opposition Party. So you went away without any trouble. Behind you followed the cheers. It was death. That stoning led to many deaths of motorists. Pedestrians. Workers. Jobless. Men. Women. Boys. Girls. It led to looting. Shops were looted. Supermarkets too. The whole of the glass got smashed. One looter had a hammer. Man. Never in your life attend a mass of a dead politician. And perhaps with a political motive behind it. You may join him on his way to paradise. Many helped T.J. to paradise. They escorted him. I nearly joined him myself. A rock of stone landed on the back of my head. When I came to my senses my pockets were empty. Some pickers know the right time to work. They pick even the dead. And they were everywhere. Back in my senses I dragged myself back to the Slums. Blood still smelled. Blood of death. And it was shed. Women were raped. It was a tribal war. It was a challenge. By sticking a pin in the eye. His death was a pin in the eye. A tribal challenge. But it was a mistake. It planted the bad evil seed, splitting the harmony and unity of tribes. His death has only brought mistrust between the tribes. Because T.J. was a man of the people. He was liked and loved by all. He died a hero's death. It was death in the street. He gave us nothing but history. He is now history. In the Slums we still mourn him. That was the last time I went to the church. I swore never to attend any mass. Never a church.

In the evening, back, out poured the events of last night. There was a dance in the hall by the Hi-Fivers and they were introducing a new dance called Kibushi. This group made girls crazy here when they came in, and some of them now have their sons and daughters. The girls used to fight each other, claiming them. Very funny. So at the dance there were fights. John had his with Njambi over their baby son. He had found out that the girl was fooling around with

115

a slob, a man of two wives, just to keep her going with fashions. So John wanted his baby boy.

But where will he take the boy? asked Burma.

We wonder, we all said. And that was because in the place where he was accommodated six more boys shared the room with him. They all squeezed together on the floor. And more, he was jobless.

Then there was the fight between the thin-legged Luise and Hadija over Josse. Luise was taking over the boy. Bi Hamida approached Burma and told him that she wanted to have a talaka, a Muslim divorce, so that she and Burma could marry. We laughed at that. Where will I take her? asked Burma. Where shall we sleep? I got no job and I got no money nor house, he explained. She is mad, said Odongo.

Then Abiba fought Mamu over Mwai, and Comby got raped by the Watalii gang. The dance ended that way. As we were still in our talk, came Hussein from Shauri Moyo, the city of the leaning trees. With him came the news of the boys who were picked up at Burma or Oboka, a nickname for the market. The boys and the traffickers in bangi were all taken in the afternoon, he said.

By whom? we all asked.

Just by a lady who is a druggist and a customer there, he said. She used to come there and buy the stuff daily so that we all thought she was just one of us. But today she was different. She came, and before the boys could wink they were all surrounded from the sewers of Kaloleni to Gor Mahia Road. Both gates of the market and the whole place was covered so that no one could escape, he said. Then the woman started unearthing the stuff. They were all surprised at how she could do that. Kirio tried to be rude and the woman gave him one on the cheeks, he added.

Why do they trust women? asked Burma. They are devils.

And then Owuor had an accident with a train, he said. He lost a leg and a foot and nearly died.

That hurt us. We said nothing. Then while we were still seated came this guy Pirate Ladino with a group of six girls. He had on a khaki suit well starched and with many holes in it. His head was clean shaved. We laughed at him and thought that he was crazy.

We knew that he was coming for a drug. He was a customer too. Seeing us, he brought the girls to us. Hi men, he said. Hi, we roared back. Then followed the introductions. The ladies seemed to enjoy that. The names were Lolly, Anne, Mary, Lolita, Betty and one said Ladino. Then ours followed, Brazze called himself Black Christ, it made them cover their mouths to hide smiles. A.J. Professor Burma, Hussein Tongolo Mbili, Uha Camara Laye, Yossa Tabu, Odongo Juma, Ali Mouse, Dan, Franco, Chubby Kassinyesto, Eddy Chura, Amasco, Urai, Bez, Pocomoco, Mkora, Salim, Jabbir, Abbasi, Supperi and Mbiraro. Also Kadugunye, Yusuf, Suleimani and Kesho, who had joined us when they saw the women. They said glad to meet us. Then they were introduced to the drug. Brazze handed a few to Lolita to try. She spat it out. It was bitter to her mouth. Mary too spat from the sticks by Burma. She chewed the karafuu cloves and got the sour taste. Odongo gave Lolita a white sweet to flavour her mouth. Pirate laughed it off, and so did we. They all bought sodas to sweeten their mouths. After buying the stuff they all left, wishing us a happy time. The handicapped Kassinyesto too wished them a nice one.

Puffers, we thought.

Women must be smoking the stuff bad these days, we said.

It is their liberation, said Odongo.

Yeah, we all agreed.

With evening already there we left and scattered to meet in alleys and paths.

5

It was Monday morning and the starting day for the month of Ramadhan. Most of the women were clad in buibuis. Some wrapped up to the tops and bridges of their noses. Some looking through the face net on the buibuis. It was a sign of fasting to every Muslim all over the world. Men were in their kanzus and tarabushis. Some in their vikoyis wrapped around the waist, and in sandals. On their faces the gloomy signs of the torture of this month. Young women in khangas. And there was quietness all over. The highest volume of noise was from here. This damn Katanga Base. The place where the boys were all false nuts. I mean those who claimed to be Muslims. They were false because they didn't fast. On the face of it you would think they did. And that was because the whole day their mouths looked dry. After they had eaten they dried the mouth. In the evening they were all at the mosque waiting for mwathini to announce the prayer and then start eating those mushkaki, drinking orange juice, kaimatis, samosas, mahamris crumbs. That was at six in the evening. From then on all the rest followed, the drinking. Then the dakku at midnight. That was the heavy meal to keep you going till the next evening. A month in which any slight exchange of words and abuse would be condemned. So we sat with nothing to do, and talk about this month came up. Burma claimed that true Muslims were gone from this place.

It is not like it was before, added Odongo. The faith in this religion is fading. People are doing one thing or the other, he added.

Who said that in this place people are fasting? asked Suleiman.

Hakuna watu wa dini Majengo siku hizi, said Yossa. No religious people.

Siku hizi ni kula kana na kuwaka. Eating and drinking, said Jabbir.

I wonder what will happen if war starts, I said.

Why, *kwa nini*? asked Ali.

Vijana wote walevi, all youths are drunks, I said.

Our freedom, said Burma. *Uhuru wa maskini*. Poor people's freedom.

Hakuna Kitu kingine ni ulevi tu, added Brazze. Nothing else but drinking.

Tutafanya nini? asked Mayanja. We are poor, what else should we do?

Ponda raha kufa kwaja, commented Pocomoco. Today he was on sick leave. Enjoy before you die.

Dunia inajaa maovu, said Kadugunye. The world is full of evils.

I will never fast, said Hussein.

I will not fast either. Let Mohammed himself do it, Jabbir said.

I'm a communist, remarked Burma. And soon I think I may emigrate to Korea. There they don't have anything to do with religions. They hate priests.

That is the place to live, I said. The Koreans know very well that any American is a liar. And no missionaries are needed there.

Mtaa huu inajaa mahibilisi, commented Yusuf. Kaffirs only.

Haki ya Mungu, truth of god, agreed Burma. Kaffirs only. And then they talk about fasting here. Who are worse sinners than the Muslims of this place?

Hakuna, none, said Juma. There is no more evil place than the Slums. No evil place beats this place.

The trouble with this place is that everyone assumes himself to know more than everyone else, explained Jabbir.

And that is the mistake of waSwahili, pointed out Suleiman. That is our main mistake.

And it is why you see mothers competing with their daughters, said Yusuf. They still claim to be teenagers.

For example that Councillor Amina and her gang, said Burma. Who is running her nowadays?

Aga Han, said Jabbir. Eddy and Hussein got their contract terminated. We laughed and so did everyone.

In the Slums there are no secrets, said Odongo.

But what is wrong with those women? asked Burma.

Who knows, answered Brazze. Perhaps their money.

WaSwahili, hatari, said Uha. They are dangerous.

I can't marry a Swahili woman, said Burma. They know too much.

Don't marry anyone, said Brazze.

They are all the same, added Yusuf. Any of them will tell you that she has been with Mama Amina while all the time she has been with a neighbour.

Just like that Fatuma, said Jabbir.

That one is too much. She is giving it to everyone, said Yossa.

I wonder what is wrong with her man, Juma wondered.

Kachumbari, perhaps. She must have played some witchcraft on that man, Burma said.

That is it. Just imagine how tough that guy was before he took her on. The guy was tough, man, said Brazze.

Very, agreed Yossa, but look at him now.

Pengine alirambishwa, commented Yusuf. Perhaps he licked it, the ash.

Never trust any woman, any figure that bends when urinating, said Brazze.

I will never trust any, vowed Burma. That one, Delilah, shaved Samson for the kill.

Then the subject changed. We talked about Israel and the Arabs. Burma spoke on it. The Arabs will never win any war with Israel, he said.

Why? asked Kesho.

They have no radar. A hungry slob sold the radar to the Israelis. It was flown by helicopter, said Burma.

Some nuts are really crazy, remarked Yossa. Imagine selling a radar.

Then the heat of the topic went up when Ghalib, as others call

120

him, but he called himself Albi, joined us. He was an Arab. Most of his time he was busy with that Yasmin. He criticised Sadat. He is not fit for that leadership, he said. Nasser was the only fit guy for it.

And what caused his death? asked Brazze mockingly.

Anything caused it. It could be heart failure or poison, he answered.

How? asked Burma. Others listened.

Corruption. People are corrupted. You see, there was one top-ranking officer in the army, I think a commander. This nut was bought and out the whole secret of the army went. All to the Israelis. Another sold out the radar, and then another one too was bought. He too sold it all out. That is when the war began on the border. When the Vice-Commander was told about it, he thought it was all a joke. He said that their war with Israel was an old war. He went on playing cards. When he came to find out that it was no joke, some parts were already captured. He committed suicide. Such things could have caused heart failure to Nasser, explained Albi.

And how about that Gaddafi? asked Brazze.

That man is sick. He is a money-sick fellow. He doesn't know what he is talking about. He thinks that he can lead the Arab world, said Albi.

Can't he lead? asked Yusuf.

Never. Not the Arabs. Only some but not all. Those whom he can buy.

You mean like that Big Daddy? asked Brazze.

That is it. That one was bought with millions he had in Geneva, and then military aid, said Burma.

Aren't those experts Black Septembers? I asked.

They are, agreed the boys. They are.

So in your mind whom do you favour most for that presidency? asked Brazze.

I think some day one of Nasser's sons will take it. The one in the army, said Albi.

Mkora, who had gone to the toilet and missed all that, came back. Like Albi, he attacked the Americans. What can Nixon do

121

without the German-Jewish Dr Kissinger? That product of Harvard University? Americans are useless without the non-Americans. The richest people are mostly the Israelis, their scientists are all foreigners. Who are the Americans? I vote for Mao, and the Russians. They never boast of their power. Their lunar missions all land back on earth. And we only hear of them when they have come back, after the completion of the mission.

And with that we got down to business as a few cars rolled in. We worked, and as more cars rolled in everyone could be seen sweating and breathing in or blowing out of his nose. We worked till evening and no more cars came. We stored the rags.

From Katanga Base and the crumbs eaten after mwathini had allowed the eating, the pagans like me all met in the stores of Masandukuni. That was after being at Mama Atieno's. In the store were Dan, Mwaura, Franco, Saidi, and Kanji Bhai. The rest of the faces were also familiar ones. Among the women were Sera, sitting in a corner. Beside her a Sanyo radio with tearabu music on. In her hands a mirror. And applying lipstick to her lips. The oldest of the women, too. She had a part in a movie and since then she is lousing around and getting kicks from the boys. Getting our orders we sat to sip them. As we were sipping the contents slowly in came these tramps Wangare and the other Sera. With them Susy. Pity. We said nothing to them. They were all parasites. That was our habit. We were so mean with our money. The hard-earned money. And they knew it. Then in came Burma. He saw them. The tarts. He mocked them. *Poleni kwa saumu*, he told them. Sorry for the fasting.

Tushapoa, we are too, they answered. They looked at us with begging eyes: Can't you, any of you, offer us one? Burma sat and took his order too.

Do you really fast? he asked them.

Why shouldn't we? answered Susy.

I doubt it, he said.

How about you? asked Sera.

I'm a Korean. I'm a pagan waiting for his day, he answered.

And so are we, that was Wangare.

But who is really interested in fasting? asked Susy. As for me, I can't.

And who is fasting in the Slums here? asked Wangare.

You Muslims, said Dan, who had joined us.

To hell with religion, said Burma. The true Muslims are no longer in the Slums.

Which ones? asked Susy.

The ones who used to dance chakacha. Those were the real ones, said Dan.

How about now? asked Sera.

Now remain Wameru, Wanandi and the rest who claim to be fasters.

The ones whom you will never hear them call themselves by their surnames. It is always Asman Ramathani or Fatuma Bakari, but never Abu Kamau or Fatuma Wanjiro. Not even Fatuma Gogo, said Burma.

Then asked Susy: Why are the others not speaking? Meaning us.

They have nothing to talk about, said Burma. After all, what do you want them to talk about?

Anything, said Wangare.

Then I felt like giving them a bomb, but refrained.

Maybe, said Susy. It is part of metric. Things have gone metric.

But you women of this place, who will marry you? asked Burma.

Our days are gone, said Susy.

Mna taabu sana nyinyi wanawake wa Majengo. Afadhali mtaa huu ubomolewe. You have troubles, you women. They better demolish this place, said Burma.

Why? asked Wangare.

It will save many lives.

What do you mean?

I mean like you sitting here now waiting for the slobs. How much do you charge them for a night? asked Burma.

A pound, answered Susy.

Kweli mna taabu. Umaskini. You sure have troubles. Poverty, said Dan.

Then the ladies left us for their hunting. Wangare at least had hooked an old slob. We pitied them and their lives. Poor them. Then the topic of the All African Trade Fair came up. It was all about how people got drunk. The women from different countries and their way of dressing. Their stands and what were good. The fashions and everything. Then the Uganda waragi. We all praised it. The manufacturing and the distillation. And then the smell of it. The topic brought it all to my memory. We had gone there a group of all the boys. We had saved enough for that purpose. Then it happened. My pocket was empty. They, sharp fingers had picked it. All the two hundred bucks. When I came to realise it, I explained it to the boys. We revenged it. Revenged it on both men and women, young and old. In that operation we netted two thousand shillings. That was enough. We then took our places at the Uganda stand. We took the distilled one. The waragi. We got drunk. Totally. Then it started. The vomiting. I vomited and vomited. At last I started crying. I cried mama and dad, and what and why did I take myself to drinking. Man. I cried. The real tears. How we got back after the boogy at that Nami's Club, I don't know.

While we were still boozing, this old nut began. He was drunk, but he knew what he was talking about. He roared: we must occupy three thirds of the Parliament seats. The cabinet ministries. We must control the whole of the government because it is we who lost blood when fighting the British for uhuru. We lost our wives and children, men, and our property. We spilt blood. It is we who brought the uhuru, he went on. None of his friends answered him. They all had their eyes to the ground. All the attention rested on this slob. He then went on: we must rule for twenty years before any other uncircumcised man rules us. We would rather die than be ruled. We still have the weapons we used in the struggle and our men are still in the forest.

Then one of the slobs asked him: What are they doing while others are enjoying the fruits of uhuru? Who do they want to fight?

124

There is war coming, he said.

And who were you fighting against, in the forest? asked another.

The British. Who else? he answered.

But you didn't fight them, you were just fighting among yourselves, and taking away other people's properties, explained another.

That hurt him. He tapped his forehead with his finger. He told the fellow that he was lucky. Had he had his weapon the guy wouldn't have seen the new day. That remark had really hurt him. A vein stood out on his forehead. Breathing was hard for him. Tears rolled down his cheeks. Then I thought about this nut. Perhaps he was a victim of the war. He must have lost plenty of his property. And perhaps he was not enjoying the fruits he expected like others. Or was he here to scare us from drinking? But why? We are just the same, in the same category. The poor common man's category. A man who was only having fun of his sweat. Who is interested in war? Not me. I hate war like anyone else. It is the end of everything. And everybody is only having fun in his time. The highest and the poorest. Kings and peasants. Killers, thieves, madmen, the same men and women. All are having fun in their time because an end comes. Who needs a civil war? It happened in Congo and worst of all in Nigeria. So who needs that pain? The pain of hunger and eating rats? The pain of jumping over the bodies of the innocent dead? The pain of seeing the naked tortured women amputated, with breasts missing? The innocent children? Crying and dying because of food? And all the time the white man laughing and poking each other's ribs and saying, see Mr Brown, I told you the black men are still in darkness. They think that having a free state is eating bread and butter. Yes, Mr Rogers. See how the blacks are having it just because of poverty. I told you, give him that freedom he is claiming for and soon he will want us back. He will want our security and our money. I told you the blacks can't rule themselves. They are still hungry. Who wants all that? Why doesn't such a man see? Perhaps an Ibo who was a victim in Nigeria during the Biafra civil

125

war can have a good answer to that man. No one in Nigeria thinks of war now. It is still in their eyes and in their dreams.

We left the Masandukuni bar because of the hot air of the slobs. We feared arrest also. It had no licence.

In the morning, sitting on this skeleton of a Renault, we went over the stories of last night. Most of the boys didn't sleep in the cars. They had invitations to go and have dakku in some houses. Some of the socialist families invited the boys they preferred. Hussein and I in turn went to the Councillor. Burma had spent it at Mwana Isha's. Her husband was on a safari. So the whole morning got wasted like that. The fasters in buibuis, the women. Others in khangas. The old men in kanzus and vikoyis and tarabushis and vilembas. They sat at the entrance of the mosque. They chatted about their old past times, their lovers, some lying, sleeping because of hunger, and one or two sewing the decorations on the tarabushis ordered for Idd Ul Fitir after the completion of the fasting. Idd is had when the moon shines after the days of fasting. It is the holiday for the Muslims all over. That day you will see them in new outfits. Just like Christmas to Christians. Everyone in his best.

After noon with the hot sun we sat under our usual spots. The gatty-chewing was not in its usual form. The boys feared the curses of the old ones. But under lips it went on. *Mtume ni nani?* Burma would question anyone who asked him the reason why he was chewing. Who is the Prophet? With nothing much to talk about and the steam of the dope in our skulls, we sat and watched the commotions of the fasters. Some had started going to Gikomba market for the dakku dish to be. The cooking started going in the evening after the bellowing of mwathini. Sometimes even before. We watched the scene. At the taps in a long file stood the debes for water. Abbasi and Marenya waited. They were for sale around the Slums. While Marenya waited he inhaled from this mangata cloth. He was inhaling the petrol. On top would be mashada. The pure dope. And then his scenes would follow. Walking out, urinating and pointing it at the women. Or acting like Tarzan, carrying a knife and hunting for dogs. He would cry out,

Tarzan-like, and charge the dog. The dogs here feared him. They knew his smell because he didn't wash. He slept in the wambazas of the Arab shops. In the corridors. Sometimes he would make a dive as if swimming. He would then bang his stomach on the road. We watched. Near the wall behind Marenya lay a black dog peacefully sleeping. The heat was too much for it to move. Some time back it was chewing some butchery papers. Those which had the stink of the meat smell. Burma remarked on it, *Hata mbwa yule anafunga*. The dog too is fasting. That made us laugh.

Then passing us on her way to toilet was this old-time woman, Kibibi. We talked about her about the beauty of her during her time. She was the queen of that group, the same group as the toothless Kadogo. Every slummer who thought he was a Casanova wanted her. She, knowing it, played the part of 'I am not cheap, man'. She was at that time for Massengo, the famous guitarist. And the worst homo. We talked of the chain of men who had been to her. The list was endless. And even up to now, she was still the lady Madonna in her prime. She didn't grow old. With her to the toilet she carried a Kimbo tin. I spat at that thought. Then, running, following her, was Kadogo. They must have eaten a lot of dakku last night. They were now going to share the water in that tin. They would be washing, facing each other, and talking about the man each had last night.

We sat and went on chatting all about the scene. Then came this crippled woman, Anne. She had got off at the bus stop near the hall and was now crossing to the city of leaning trees. Seeing her brought all the memories to my mind. And I vowed never again to trust a crippled woman. I wanted that stunted woman Temmy and the easy way was through this talkative cripple, because they were neighbours. I trusted her to do it and she in return promised and assured me that she would do it. How silly I was. Temmy was her brother's girl.

Anne assured me that Temmy was willing to agree to be my girl. And all the time she knew that her brother was running her. When I came to meet Temmy she said no, her time of love was not yet. That she was still a virgin. My God. Do you know what I came to find out after that? It was all bullshit. Before anyone else, she was an ex-girl of Singh. And still this crippled woman went on bullying me with false promises. I spat when I saw her. Never again will I trust a cripple or any women.

Then while we were still seated in rolled two cars. A blue Toyota and a white Ford Escort. We watched them. New customers. No. In the white Ford was Zakia. My God. We watched them park and get out. I grinned and approached them. One of those in the Toyota was a slim tall woman with sunglasses on. The other was short and stout. Hello Eddy, said Zakia. The others stood watching.

Hello, I said back. Hussein came and joined me.

Hello, said Hussein to them. They answered. Then they called me aside from Hussein and told me that the cars needed washing and while that went on they wanted me to take them around. My friends want to see the place, explained Zakia. I looked at them and they all grinned. Not bad, I said. I issued the order to Hussein and took the ladies around. Passing the mosque they wondered at the old men sleeping at the gate. Why do they do this? asked the slim tall one.

It is a good resting-place, I said. No disturbance or pickpockets.

And why are all the women I have seen clad in this black garment? What do they call it? asked the stout one.

Buibui, I said.

Why are they wearing it? she asked.

Because they are fasting. It is the month of Ramadhan, I said.

Oh, I see, she said.

And how about you? Are you also fasting? asked Zakia.

No, I'm not a Muslim, I said.

I thought you were, she said.

No, I said.

Sorry, Eddy, I didn't introduce you to my friends. Sorry, she apologised.

It is okay, I said.

This one, introducing me to the tall slim one, is Janet and this one is Mrs Olu. All my friends. Janet is with the bank and Olu with the coffee firm.

That is good, I said. I'm Eddy, and I grinned at them.

That is good, they roared. We moved towards Sophy. There I explained to them about the drug, miraa. We passed the headquarters of the Black Stars, the TV comedians. So they come from here? asked Olu.

Yeah. Just from here, I said.

Those people are really good, she said. I like them on TV. We went towards the Maternity, to Eastleigh, and turned up this Hamilton Road. All the time they were talking among themselves. I looked at the mamas in this block, standing at the first and second floor windows looking out at the passers-by. They envied us. They had eyes that said 'men are nothing but beasts'. They like us but at the times of labour you don't see them. They were all pregnant and looking at the men with hate. Sorry, mamas, I said inwardly.

My women too looked at them. Then I heard Olu commenting something about the place and the worst of men when you are pregnant. You don't see them. They leave the pain to women. I felt happy inside. Then came the question which was like a bomb to me. And it was from Zakia. Do you know any waSwahilis who are *waganga*? That was it. Witchdoctors. In the Slums they are known as Sharrifs. Most of them are cheats, liars. What they do is all shit. I wondered when people will realise the truth about them. They would read to you from a Koran type of book, tell you to bring a black chicken for the job, give you some irizi and all the funny things that you were to use. Every day we see women coming to them, all beautiful. The trouble with them being men.

We know all the tricks the Sharrifs use and play on them. After the huge amount of money has been received, the Sharrif would tell you, *Akili ni mali*: To live you have to have guts. He would tip you to shut your mouth, and then eat the chicken. I wished these women knew about them. All these thoughts ran through my mind. Then I said yes. I have known some. There are many of them here.

And who do you think is better than the others? asked Janet.

That depends, I said. It depends on the outcome. Whether what he does to you comes out the way you want it.

But which one do you suggest for us? asked Olu.

There is that one at Eastleigh, Sheikh Ufunguo, and that one of California. There is that one at Digo, and that one at Danguroni behind the barber's shop. Also another one at Katanga Base there.

But which one tops all? asked Janet.

Well, that will be for you to decide. But let's try the one at Danguroni. I think he is okay. That was a lie. I knew there would be a tip. That one was the worst. He was known all over as the worst Sharrif. It has even come out that his last wife, Saidi's mother, left him or took her talaka because of his evil deeds. Two previous wives had done the same thing.

Okay, they agreed. We went there.

At Sharrif's place there were few people. Perhaps they knew of his lies or didn't see any good come of it. We waited in the outer room because there was a customer inside. After some time she came out. She was a lady. Another sufferer, a prisoner of love. No man wants her. Her boy must be a liar, I thought. He must have promised her marriage but has changed his promise to another tramp. Too bad for the ladies. What a beautiful spring chicken to be in that trouble! I felt pity for her. She looked lost. Completely lost. Her time was running out and nobody was paying any attention to her. I thought, Woman, why don't you pick on me and feed me? I will be true to you for the rest of my time. Then I entered the inner room and found Sharrif. He must have collected a large sum from that woman. *Hodi ndani*, I said.

Karibu, come in. *Ooh, Chura, mbona unapotea?*

Taabu, I said. Visitors for you.

Who are they? he asked.

Women of money, I answered.

Bring them in, he said.

I went out and called them. We all went in and they got themselves seated.

Sharrif greeted them. How are you all?

Fine, they answered. How are you?

130

Fine, answered Sharrif.

Thank you, they said.

Well, began Sharrif. Your problems?

That was it. They felt ashamed because of me. But Sharrif told them not to worry, that I was very faithful and reliable. But they still had some doubts about each other, I thought. The Sharrif told them to wait in the outer room. We remained, I and Zakia. Out poured the problems. Her husband was cheating her with some tarts, he wanted to boot her out because she could not produce. After listening to her, the Sharrif assured her that it was simple. That the requirements were a black cock, an egg, some of his pubic hair and a cloth with his dried sperm on it. These would then be mixed together with some other herbs and burned together. The ashes from it she would pour in her husband's tea. She would then have by her an irizi and she would only need to mention her husband's name and wherever he was he would come running home. After that he read some of the writings from his book in Arabic. My lady understood nothing. When he had finished, she paid thirty shillings examination fee. Then came Janet. Her problem was the same. Her husband. The same thing was told to her. The same fee. And the same with Olu. I pitied them and thought of them and their unknowing husbands. People, I thought. Problems and nothing but problems. God forgive the poor souls.

We left the Sharrif's house and headed back to Katanga Base. On the way we discussed nothing. Perhaps each one was thinking of what the Sharrif had said. The fee for the whole job would be three hundred each, the Sharrif had said. That was no worry to them, they said. After all, what is money? What is money if not used? To have a good life or save money?

At Katanga, the cars were all ready. They paid twenty and drove off. Going back to Sharrif was up to them, I said. I don't want to be there. That is their trouble. We split the pound, I taking only five from it. And that was because in my pocket was a pound tip from the Sharrif. Then the mwathini bellowed. That saved me from questioning. Otherwise it would have been bad. We all stored the rags and waited for those who were praying prayers to finish.

This was when all the fasters were allowed to wet their mouths. And to false Muslims like us it was the same. We then fell on the crumbs. The people in buses looked at us and wondered to themselves what was wrong with the mob down there at the mosque? Some envied us for the crumbs. They were all tired from their daily jobs with no profit at all at the end. From the mosque we went towards Digo with our mushkaki cuds in our cheeks. Then I told Hussein what had happened. The tall slim one works with the bank, I said. The short stout one is the wife of a Permanent Secretary.

And what was wrong with their husbands? asked Hussein.

They were cheating them. So was Zakia's. Her man wanted to get rid of her because she didn't produce, I said.

The nut. What are children for nowadays? he asked.

But for them it's okay. They have responsible jobs, I said. They have money and all that.

It is up to them, he spat.

And do you know how much the Sharrif is charging them? I asked.

Which Sharrif? asked him.

Omari, I said.

Mahalim? he asked.

Yeah, I said.

How much then? he asked.

Three hundred each, I said.

Well, that is okay. They have money, let the Sharrif suck them, he sighed.

I wished they had known about that Mahalim. They would hate him to death. I wished they knew how the Sharrif was chased from the Coast. I wished they knew the secret that the Sharrif was the man between in every controversy between a man and his wife. How he used to cheat a wife that he was only the man who was planting the seeds of love in the woman to make her husband love her more, while all the way he was making use of his time. In turn the husband would go to him about his wife and be told that the only way to do it was to kick out the wife because there are so many women running after men. And the wife would then run to him

132

as the only man who could help her. Mahalim is a real Sharrif. A man of guts. And that's how he earns his living, I explained.

Why worry about all that? he asked.

I'm not worrying, I said.

Then?

Then nothing. I'm only worried about women, the way things are turning against them, I said.

What do you mean? he asked.

Like those women now, what is it they miss? They are well off, having top husbands, cars and money. And still they are not happy, I said.

Yeah, that is how things are. Money is nothing. Love matters, he said.

But they have love, I said.

No. They are the worst people, full of troubles. What type of women do you see going to Sharrif? he asked.

Nearly all kinds. International prostitutes, women with schemes, wives of ministers, top bosses and all, I said.

And that is how their lives are. They all depend on and believe in those superstitions. They are all chained to it. He spat aside.

So after all we, the local nuts, are okay, I said.

We are, yes. Very much so. You see, with them, they are afraid to lose all the riches they have. You, what can you be afraid of? he asked.

Nothing, I said.

And that is why you don't go to Sharrifs.

Still moving on, we came upon a quarrel between Kerera and his woman Amina, slummers. They were quarrelling because Kerera had heard a tip that this Amina was fooling around with some musician. On Amina's back she carried a young child, the third of their four children. We passed them and went ahead. That was a husband and wife affair, we thought. It was a scene you could see here every day between the boys and their girls. The next minute you would see them laughing together. At Digo there was another scene. Thick black smoke curling to the sky. We rushed to it. It was as I thought. Fire. The slums of Santa Maria were on fire. That was the whole shit of building a slum with paper and plastic. One catches fire and the whole row burns. So Santa Maria was on fire. We stood at the corner of the Digo Road and watched the Kitui Village, as it is sometimes called, burning. The villagers were fighting the flames hard but they were too much for them. Also most of them were already drunk. It must be one of the drunks who did it. He must have taken a lot and thrown away a butt without caring. It could even have been Lord Zangaro. But no, it couldn't have been him. By now he would be on the table in the snooker room, gambling. The flames flared up more. The efforts of the villagers were useless. They couldn't put the fire out. The helpless mothers stood and watched all their belongings in flames. The babies were crying on their backs. Their black dogs too sensed danger. They stood afar with the watchers. Then we heard it. The Fire Brigade sirens. They were coming at a terrific speed. We made way for their big tankers. Behind them trailed the ambulance, its siren too blaring. The fight began. Water against fire. The pipes throwing their holders this way and that way. The power of water was strong. The engine running, pumping the strength out. They fought. At last the water won. Now remained only the smoke from the burnt-out beds and worn-out tatters. The villagers looked around for the leavings. The damage was immense. Among what was lost were the illegal brews, changaa and munyeki, plus the dope, gabba. We left and took to our daily routine. The whole of the Slums was talking about the fire in Santa Maria. Some were saying, last time it was Mathare Valley, now it is Santa Maria and twice before the Gikomba market, now which one will follow? I asked Hussein, too, which one would be next. Guess, he said.

The Slums. Those wrecks, our homes, will be the next. Then where shall we have it?

What?

Our nap.

Along the streets of River Road.

Those who live there won't let you, unless you are one of them. Never, I said.

What shall we do, then? he asked.

Looks like we will take to the graveyard. The only place with

134

no molestation. They won't let you stay in the mosque for long. If they find out, I mean the waSwahili, you will be out that very minute. They won't even let me into the church. Perhaps the priest thinks that I'm after the candles and the brass. Or even the statue of that nut fellow of a Christ, I explained.

It's nothing to worry about now. Wait till it happens. Then we shall know, he said.

It was Wednesday morning, and no business at all, only Bez and Urai doing a station-wagon Peugeot. Burma, in an army jacket and cap he bought recently, making him look like a Cuban revolutionary with his untrimmed beard, leaning on this skeleton of a Renault; Njoroge on this tree reading the latest Flamingo; Brazze talking to this eye-doctor; Kadugunye selling dope to this Patty tourist driver; Hussein nowhere to be seen; Rajab holding this supposed son of his, and knowing very well that the father was a councillor who took his girl to bed to secure her a job with the Council; I doing nothing with the rest of the boys, when there was this loud noise from the direction of the Chief's camp.

We looked in that direction but saw nothing, only the dust. We saw the people running in that direction. We all followed. The taxi drivers too. Then at this Kabete Ushujaa Tailor shop we found the mob. A Peugeot saloon was on its back with its wheels to the sky and a shattered screen. Two people in the trench. An accident. On the door step stood Mariamu, clutching her baby girl, the baby she tried to kill in the abortion attempt. We watched the scene. Moving around it was this thief, Mbithi. The driver was not to be seen, and that was why Mbithi was making the best use of the time. While everyone was watching the scene the battery would go missing or the jack, the spare wheel tyre, or anything of value for use in cars. He never missed something to pick up. The sympathising Samaritans held one of the injured fellows in a position where he could breathe, and so with the other one. We started off back. On the way we met with the driver of the car. A very young chap who couldn't have been the owner of it. He was held tight by this administration police. Otherwise he would have got it from the Public Law. A sound beating. They cursed him. *Bahati yako*, they said. You are very lucky. They pointed their fingers at him. We sat for the next twenty minutes or half an hour before we heard the ambulance siren. Shit you, we cursed them. It takes them very long to come to the scene of an accident, complained Burma. Last time the woman died because of that. They were late, otherwise she wouldn't have died, he continued. We talked of the accidents on this road. It had become a black spot. That saloon might have killed the tailors, said Bez. And that Masai was lucky. He had nothing on him of value, otherwise on coming back to his senses he would have died of heart failure. Those pretending to be Samaritans are the worst pickers. Nowadays they even rob the dead, remarked Kadugunye.

The whole morning went on with nothing else happening. Then while we were waiting for business under the shade, with the fasters yawning now and then with hunger and the dust disturbing us from Nandi Street, from Danguroni, suddenly in rolled this dark blue Benz. We all stared at it. It was not known here. A new customer. We looked at him and then looked at each other. Man. It was rather strange. We all gaped at him. On his head was this beaded cap. On his chin the beard. He got out. With him was this never-left-behind fly-whisk. Clad in this communist fashion, khaki knee-length trousers, and on his feet the Akamba shoes. Akalla. He was Ja-Nam, the former leader of the banned Opposition Party. It was only recently that he had come out of detention, after being detained when the general election was due. A very complicated matter. He was a communist. He was still not in his old form. He was slim. The word had gone around like a bush-fire, and a mob started to gather. He, too, was a man of the people. And a very world-wide famous chap. The gathering mob stood afar as if not aware of his presence. But all the time coming closer and closer. He then came towards us and greeted us: *Jamboni wananchi*? How are you, citizens?

Hatujambo Mheshimiwa, we roared back. We are fine, your honour.

He then went on, I want my car washed, who will do it?

No one was bold enough to admit they would do it, after being gripped with respect.

136

Each one looked at his friend as if saying, okay, who now?

Then Burma volunteered. I will do it, your honour.

He then said no more. He stood under the shade of a tree and waited for the job to be finished. Uha was not around, so Burma called me to give him a hand. Together we did it. The mob now came nearer him. Among them was this Mama Uhuru woman. A famous woman around here and a woman who had really enjoyed the minister's money during the campaign. She had no husband but many bastards. She approached him. *Habaro yako Mheshimiwa?* she asked. How are you, your honour?

He grinned at her. They were familiar to each other.

Very fine, he said, shaking her hand.

Then she added *Pole*, sorry. Meaning, for his detention.

It's okay.

Come in, she invited.

Thank you, but I'm in a hurry, he answered.

He then looked at the assembled mob, the taxi-men, the boys and everybody. He said nothing to them. They stood mum, but adoring him. We hurried on with his car and finished it in no time. He didn't ask the charge. He produced his wallet and handed us a pound note and got in. He then looked at us as if wondering about us and what the damn hell the government was thinking about young men like us who were doing nothing but lazing and fooling about with washing cars. With that he whistled at us and rolled away. That started us talking about him. His work when he was a minister for home affairs and how he used to give the whites time to leave the country after an insult by a white to a black. Sometimes he would give three hours, one hour, six hours, even half an hour to a white to pack off. That made his fame grow wide. Then came the day he resigned from the government and the party. The next morning no one wanted to board a bus on his way to work. That was because the next day he went on foot from his house into town, chatting with the wananchi and explaining to them the reasons why he had resigned his post and left the ruling party, the DP. He told them that the party had elements who were fighting hard against him. They didn't want him and were fighting for his downfall. As for the government, it had failed on its promises to the wananchi.

137

Free education and medicine and the increase of salaries to ease the heavy burden on the common man; the minimum he wanted was £20. The government didn't agree with him on that. He complained that the rich were getting richer and the poor poorer. Such things led to his resignation which added more fame to him. So when he drove away we spoke of all those things. And how perhaps the state needs such people to steer the country ahead. One day the voices of the people will want him back, they finished, and went back to their occupations.

Still at the Katanga Base, the news reached us that two of the Slums boys had been picked up. Kokroch was taken at Ngara. He entered a music shop and, as if it was his father's shop, tried to walk out with a tape recorder. The beating they gave him will remain in his bones to be felt in his old age.

Odundo was taken at River Road in a Bata shop. He had money, yes, to buy the pair of shoes he wanted. He went in to the Bata shop with sandals on his feet. He tried on a pair and, thinking that he was not being watched, he tried to walk out with them on, leaving his sandals behind. When the *Utumishi kwa Wote* arrived, he was half dead. The Public Justice: whenever I thought of it, even if I had a purse halfway to my pocket, I coiled up my fingers. The little finger of my right hand was a souvenir. In my old age I will be reminded of my deeds by it. Stealing is not a good job. I tried it and I'm standing accused of it now. We thought nothing about the picking up of the boys. They were only trying to keep pace with the moving world. Trying to survive the world of hell's pressure.

Then in the evening with every one waiting for this mwathini to bellow up, there was this roaring of a motorcade. His Excellency's escort. Leading them were the motorbike police waving aside all the cars to stop and make way for the Old Man. Ten of them, then following them four Benz with plain-clothes police. Their eyes wide open looking in all the directions. Then a blue one with a 'P.M. ESCORT' plate on its roof. Then the big bullet-proof gift from Germany. The Old Man in it, waving his fly whisk and the pointing finger, a sign of the ruling party, the DP. The mob cheered him, their fingers to the sky. The state's man.

I liked his beard. Behind him trailed another Benz with plain-clothes police. His bodyguards. Their eyes sharper than Hugo's. Then lastly the cheeky laughing female mongrels. They were laughing at us, standing watching them beside the road. I spat and, bending my middle finger, I stabbed the air with it. But shits, they didn't know its meaning. They loved me more, I thought stupidly.

The old man can't forget this place. This place has the history of the whole of Town. It is the mother of Nairobi. And that is true, though some call it a two-shilling city because of these two-shilling women, others Majengo, Pumwani, Matopeni because of the mud buildings with brown rusted roofs, or Mairungi city or Miraa because of the drug; a place where the Old Man during his teenage times was the tough nut with his friends, among them the bald headed Kaggo, in Sophia Town. Yes. That is the Slums. A city where people shit in tins at night and pour them out in the trenches in the morning. A most corrupted city. A place where evil can be seen at any time of the day but worse in the night. A place with every kind of people. The richest and the poorest. A city of no shame. A place full of many bastards. Corrupt police too. A city where evils of love are hidden in buibuis and kanzus. With both married and unmarried. A city where the youngsters you see playing naked in the dust are the leaders of tomorrow. Yes. Perhaps, yes. To me this was the Slums. One of the most independent cities. Living here takes guts.

With the motorcade gone, Burma shouted, You saw the Old Man?

Yeah, man. Still growing strong, I said.

He made me think that I was in Germany.

Why? asked Hussein.

The motorcade. Those 280Ss he replied.

His time, man. He suffered for them, said Kesho.

May God bless him, said I, pointing my fingers to the sky.

That is it, said Burma. Then bellowed the mwathini.

Thursday morning, on the first page were the two snaps of the boys. Their faces covered with black lines to avoid identity. Below

139

them followed the captions. These newspaper fellows are nosey. I thought, why waste the columns of their papers for such minor affairs? Picking up is a daily thing all over the world. There was nothing strange to it. Christ was nailed between them. So what was the publication for? After all, the slummers in such matters are known to be only trying to catch up with the widening pace of living. 'The Ordinaries', in prison terms. The natural born crooks. The tough nuts who were more happy in jails. They were cared for, guarded, free clothing and bedding, no tax and all. The cost of living to them was cheap. I wondered what was so important about it to that publication. Great men do it. Moore was got during a tour to Mexico for a bracelet. But owing to corruption the case got dismissed by the Bogotá law. Why? Simple. A great sportsman. A nut with quids. Money. So never blame Judas. And so too the boys. They were desperate. They had no jobs because no one was willing to give them one. No one could give them one because they had no contact with the people at the top. The top guys wanted something to wet their hands, because they said that a dry palm was never licked unless wet. They needed four hundred in advance to get you a messenger's job. You have never worked before, so where the hell will the slummer boy get all that money? And when he tries his hand on the easy target, as he thought, he was picked up and then what followed was public justice and on top of all the newspaper publication with snapshots and below them the captions descrbing the game. Shit. I said shit, you men at the top. You corrupt monkeys. Again I said S.H.I.T., shit, you black monkeys. Black politicians and all. May you all live to explain, one day. I cursed and spat.

Black men at the top, you are the cause of all this shame in the eyes of the world. You want us the slummers to adore and kneel before you to make you feel great. It takes a year before the slummer gets a chance of seeing you, so that you can write him a letter to take to a firm that you have shares in. You feel proud when he shows his unwashed face at your office every morning. You aren't even ashamed to take a slum woman for a bed interview to get her a job of cleaner in your office, so that you can take her to bed any time you want as a change from your wife. Shame on you

140

all. You are the proof of the incapability of blacks. The roots of corruption. That is what you are. To save the good things for your children. The jobs, the money and everything. But watch out. Watch, ministers, councillors and all the top men. Watch out. One day the cards will be turned against you and the worst will fall upon your children. Today me, tomorrow you. Watch out. Those chains and strings of businesses you own from the sweat of down-at-heel common men and beggars, you will vomit them up. It is only a matter of time and patience. You don't want us and are always introducing new laws, 'Vagrants Acts', because you are afraid of us and do not want to see us. But we will avenge it on your children. Yes, that will be. No joke.

You destroy their homes, the mud, plastic, paper homes, and leave them homeless with their young on their backs crying because of the pain, while you, you are laughing the next day, seeing how their homes were burning to ashes with them gloomily sitting, watching helplessly, because the police are standing there with batons and shields to bar them from rescuing their only possesions. Laugh, and call them, *Waafrika maskini*. The poor Africans. Forget that in those Slums every day burnt to ashes are the leaders of tomorrow. Forget that. Things change. They are the brainy chaps because they are being brought up to live under hardship. They don't eat eggs with butter every morning like your children. Among them are the writers, politicians, officers, broadcasters, great sportsmen, revolutionaries and everything. The intellectuals. Molest them, swoop down on them in raids, because they are a menace to the tourists, whom you are second best to. Those tourists don't swoop down on beggars and cripples around their own Hiltons. They give them help.

Kick them and spit on them. But men, watch it. Watch it, because the Common Man will take over. Within a short time you will tell him how you got the millions you have. You will sleep at the end of the bed. That is when you will know that it is cold at the end of the bed. You won't cheat him any more with false promises with no foundation. They are sick up to the neck. You won't cheat them with tribal ideas, because they are sharing the slum life and the poverty. Watch out. It is only a matter of time.

141

Perhaps they are vultures. The vulture is a patient bird, they say. But one day . . . Don't be surprised to find yourself talking alone on the streets. Don't wonder if you die in exile. Never wish for the times that are gone, because they won't come back. Your deeds will be in the open. And what will you do? You will look down, resting your chins on your chests, dropping tears. But no tears will come out. No tear will flow on your fat cheeks. Instead they will roll inward. They won't taste the usual taste of salt. They will be bitter and hard to swallow. They will choke you. In the meantime, grab all the money and the richness. Send the money to the world bank. Send it to Geneva. Smuggle it out. Drain the Common Man to his bones and leave him dry. Let him adore you. Let him entertain you when you set off on visits and when you come back from them. Back from visits abroad while you show the inheritance of a white man. Kissing your wives. Shit. A black knows no meaning in a kiss. Let him dance for you in the sun and rain, torturing himself foolishly, while you sip your whiskies thinking in your mind how the hell you will make him adore and fear you more. How you will get rid of him. Let him torture himself at Santa Maria, Kamukunji, the Park, Bangla Desh or the Kariobangi and Mathare slums. Think how you will pass a law to burn him down and force him to come and kneel before you. Be Kings. Burn his homes because they are filthy and spread epidemics. Wind up your car windows when you pass through them. See your doctors when you reach home after passing through them, because of the dust blowing in. Neglect him. It is only a matter of time, I repeat. Investigations will be carried out into the chains and strings of businesses you possess. This has been done before and it will be done again. Watch out on those poor men's wealth. Don't wonder about the Watergate Scandal. The Lord Lambton in London. Don't wonder about Nixon in the US. He is an example to you. But it will be worse in Africa. Because at the moment it is an internal lava, burning, looking for a way out. When that weak spot is found and reached it will burst out in a way that will make history. It happened to that General Ankrah in Ghana and then to Busia, but more is on the way. There are signs but you don't see them. Or you see them but just ignore them. That is it. You ignore them.

142

But they are there. See them all over the world. The Universities.
Yes, the Universities. The students' scandals. In France, Ma-
dagascar, Zaïre, Nigeria, Kenya and everywhere. So many of
them. But they are not enough. One major scandal is still in store.
And that is the worst one. The Poor Common Man Scandal. The
man who elected you to your seats in the Parliament where you are
making the best use of your time. That is the scandal that will spill
all the beans of your wealth.

In the afternoon as we were sitting under the shade came Bilali.
He was from the mosque, on his head a tarabushi and hiding his
cool, corrupt eyes were the American sunglasses. He joined us. His
404 injection was being done by Urai and Bez. I thought about
him. How corrupt he was, his smuggling job, the robberies and
raids he had committed. And now from the mosque. Shit. What
a corrupt chap this nut was. He was on the wanted list in his
country. Joining us Burma shot him a question, *Mzee kazi wapi
safari hii?*, meaning, where will he strike this time? *Bado*. Not yet.
Things are still hot. There are too many road blocks, he answered.
Then he started telling us his times during the jobs. He was in the
middle of telling us about how once he was stopped at a road block
and in his car were eight elephant tusks and three rhino's. He
nearly shitted. He knew that it was the end of his time in the
business. But he played it coolly. With his looks and personality
and the cleanliness of his car, they didn't bother to check. They
waved him through. In the middle of this story the Datsun car
entered the Base. The usual familiar faces in it. The most corrupt
nuts. Bilali saw them too. He rose and approached them. We
watched him get into the car and off they drove. That was it. At
last they had found him. There must be something on, we thought.
A raid must have been done somewhere and now they wanted some
tip from Bilali. There was some rumour that Bilali was a sort of
an informer to these guys. That was when another gang blew the
loot from a bank, a gang that was not his.

Soon after they had gone he came back. We waited for it. What
it was all about. He spilled it. That was the trouble of being known
by these guys, he said. At any raid they must come to you and

143

demand to know who did it. And that wouldn't be enough. They wouldn't let go of you unless you handed out something, he went on. They have taken five hundred from me right now, he said.

Five hundred? repeated Burma.

Yeah. Five hundred just now, the few minutes I left you sitting here.

Black shit, abused Burma. The law men. Their mothers'.

Last week on Tuesday they took from me one thousand five-hundred, said Bilali.

Why all that? asked Mayanja.

I had them. Twelve tusks. And do you know how much they were worth?

How much? asked Burma.

Twenty-five thousand, he replied.

God. That is money. But tell me which is more expensive, elephant's or rhino's? asked Burma.

Rhino is more. Once you have them, sink them into the water for two days or three. That is to let them suck water for more weight, he said.

But where do you get most of these tusks? asked Hussein.

In NFD. There everyone is on the game.

And which is more profitable, the tusks or gems? Diamonds, I mean?

There is so much involved in diamonds, replied Bilali. The story came to an end when the boys got busy.

Saturday came and I thought of the promise I had given to Grace. Telling Hussein, I left for Uplands. At the stop at this stage I looked at this building with hate at the sight of it. Mr Anam was still there with that leaking secretary. One day, man, watch it. At the roundabout I admired the beautiful sight of Lake Uhuru. I thought of the coup. It was organised here. The Parliament facing it would have come to pieces. It would have tumbled to the ground. I wondered where they would be debating about the way of dressing, as they were doing now. They wanted all the members to be in ties and jackets. What an uhuru. The Parliamentarians were like school students. You could sleep in there provided you were in a jacket and tie. You could snore and fart in there. The allowance was still there for you. The black white men. Shit. I wondered what the Chinese wore in their Parliament. I thought to myself, this liberation and uhuru was nothing but shit. We were still in the same boots and suits, the same communications, the same diplomatic service and in everything like a white man. Nothing of skins and spears and clubs. No cave living and hunting. Civilisation, that was what it was. Shit.

From my dreamland this conductor demanded his fare. I paid two shillings for the journey. At Kenyatta hospital this nut of an Ongutu fellow got in. A very crazy fellow. He believed in himself and in blackism. Always claimed that to know a woman better you had to take her into darkness. He adored Castro and Guevara. He now believed that only two things were left in this world. That was corruption and women. You corrupt yourself and then turn to a woman. That was to ease the strain on the mind. I was lucky he didn't see me when entering the bus. Past this Uthiru stop the bus was like hell. The driver must have taken a little. The bus was moving at a terrific speed. The conductor shouting to him to increase the speed. They were now competing. There was another bus at the back which wanted to overtake. Good Christ, I prayed. If an accident occurred no one would be left alive.

We stopped at Sigona Golf Club. Parked around were the cars of golfers. I took a look back to the city. Only the two tall buildings I could see. The Hilton Hotel and the KANU Headquarters. Now we left behind this Zambezi Motel. We passed all the Muguga, Kikuyu Station and the rest and came to a stop at this one Mutarakwa stop. Parked around were VW kombis, with tourists buying the local man-made handcrafts, fur hats and kiondos. Some fruits, too. We packed in more passengers so that now we were sitting three people on a chair for two. Some were standing, holding to this rail high up. Man, the heat was too much. This fat woman was breathing hard. She was pressing me to the floor of this lorry. We squeezed more on the seats. Each had four occupants now. This was worse than death. I felt like getting down for fresh air. The traffic policeman came in and roamed his eyes around. He smiled. Then, come out you, he told my next occupant. The nut tried to hide it. The butt. It had been seen long ago man. The police demanded to know why he was smoking in the bus. The nut kept mum. He then apologised for doing it. The policeman then hopped off and the damn lorry of a bus was in motion. But without the conductor. At a distance of a hundred yards or two it halted. I looked out to know why. Behind us, the conductor was coming running. He whistled and the bus started before he was even in it. He chased it and held the window rails and hopped inside. He then told us what had happened. He concluded with: It is all money nowadays. You can even kill if you have money and the file will get lost before the start of the case. And that was true, I thought. Recently the Attorney General admitted that there was something odd with the police force. So many cases had been dropped due to loss of files. Shit. With the tremendous speed of a safari car we were dropping down at Limuru, I felt good to be out of that Sauti ya Taifa. But I found something odd with this air. It was too dense. I found difficult in breathing. Well, I looked around for the UPLAND signboard. There it was. But no sign of Grace. I took a walk around to see more of the place.

It was the first time I was here. The place was famous for being cold. And I found that to be true. Everyone I saw was in a pullover, with a coat on and an overcoat. And yet the sun was shining very hot. I wondered. I looked strange to these nuts I met with. They looked at me suspiciously. Their looks were a threat to me. They scared me. I walked quickly and pretended to be a man of this place. I looked again at this signboard. She hadn't come. Shit. I hated waiting. I watched these asses pulling these carts. On them sacks. I looked at this Bata plant. It was beautiful. So that was the place where the products came from. I crossed the road and moved into the woods. Some asses were feeding here. I felt scared at the sight of two policemen. With their rifles. I couldn't see what they were guarding here. I got back to the signboard and waited for this nut of a woman. I killed time by eating oranges sold here by this old man. Then came this matatu, pirate taxi. I watched all the passengers alighting. She was not there. The next one perhaps. I waited. Then this Datsun pick-up. She was not there. I gave her more time. If two more came without her then she could say bye when she came. I waited. I waited. Then this Peugeot pick-up. No one. That was one, I said. I waited. I felt bored. I felt like hopping into one and heading back. These eyes I saw scared my heart. I waited. Now it was the last chance. If she was not in this one coming, this blue kombi, then to hell. At the stop everyone got out. No more. But . . . one more was coming out from the driver's seat. A young woman, but . . . she was in a wig. That was why I couldn't recognise her at first. She blew me a wide smile, I blew back. Hello, she said.

Hello, how are you since last time? I asked.

Fine, how about you? she asked.

Not bad, I said.

What time did you come? she asked.

Not very long, but long enough. I have walked around seeing the shops and I was about to go, I explained.

Really? she asked.

Yeah. This kombi was my last time for you, I said.

You don't mean it, she said.

I do, I said.

Then I'm lucky, just came in time, she said.

You are, I said.

So? Let's do some shopping and go back. You see, we have to do the shopping here, there the shops don't have all the things we are always in need of.

Like? I asked.

Toilet paper, bread, milk and things like cocoa and all that, she said.

And why do they put up shops there, then? I asked.

Well, they help with small commodities like fags and other things, she replied.

I see, I said.

We then took to the shops, buying the requirements. Toilet paper roll, milk, bread, toothpaste, butter and what not. We then waited for a matatu. We got into this kombi and up we went. So Uplands is some distance from Limuru? I asked her on our way.

Yeah. Perhaps six or seven miles. And not only that, where we are going to drop is another one and half miles to the place.

147

You must then be living in a bush, I said.

I told you the place is very boring, she said.

Looks like it, I said.

Just wait till we get off. This stage now is called Murangeti, she said.

Why? I asked.

It is the name for it. The one we are going to get off at is called Nyambare. From there then Uplands. We drove on.

This now is the last stage. We got off there. The matatu took its way back. Okay, she said, now the walk. This is the road leading to Matathia. It is twelve kilometres to there. You see the paths, just like those of Majengo, she said.

But these ones are okay, they have no human shit like those of Majengo, I said.

Yeah. But all the same, the place is boring me to death, she said.

You looked for a job though? I said.

I have to do it, she replied.

Then stop complaining. Tell me, what is this music from the trees?

I hate that hissing on these trees. It always scares me, she replied.

And this place seems to be too quiet, why is that? I asked.

There are no people. Most of the people around are only women, she said.

And why is that? I asked.

The men died during the Mau Mau troubles. And especially at that place Murangeti. There are more women than men.

I see. And where is this place, the famous one in the history of Kenya, this place called Lari? I asked.

Just ahead there. The place we are now approaching. You see those huts over there? she asked.

Yeah, I said.

Then around that dip where you see the cattle drinking water, she pointed out.

So that is the place the bloody massacre took place? I asked.

Yeah, she agreed.

148

And how about these barbed wire fences I see around, what are they for? I asked.

They are the acres for the remembrance of the dead. Those who were massacred, she replied.

And what caused the killing? I asked.

Suspicions. You see, those who were in the forest would not let those who were left in the villages join them. Moreover it could take you more than a month before you found those who were already in the forest. But they never allowed the left-behinds to join them. So if a left-behind went to join them they suspected him of spying. If he managed to escape, and came out again, he was counted as a Mau Mau. So it was very difficult to live in peace. Then those in the forest suspected those outside of giving them away. That was then when the massacre happened.

So it was to prevent them from giving them away? I went on.

That is it. They wanted no communication with the outside world. And that is why the place is so quiet. There are no people.

That is why the history is known all over Kenya. The Lari Massacre, I said.

Yeah. It was terrible. It spared nothing. Humans and animals, all the same. They were cut down mercilessly. I'm telling you it was horrible. I wish you could sit with one of these women around here. They never want to talk about it. It is still in their eyes, she said.

Well, as for that, it must be in somebody's eyes. The killing was very brutal.

After all, black against black. But don't you think it will happen again? I asked.

I hope it happens when I'm not around, she said.

Looks like it will happen again. I always think and feel so and this time it will be worse, I said.

What do you mean? she asked.

I mean more will be killed than at Lari. It will be the poor against the rich, I said.

I also think so, she said.

I wonder how it will be after the Old Man. This time it will be tribal, just like it happened after the death of that economy guy. When the oath-taking took place with the people in those lorries marked KANU PRIVATE. Don't you think so? I asked.

Well, may it happen when I'm not around, she said.

Where will you be? I asked.

God knows, she said.

That is it. God knows. But I never stop that imagination. After the Old Man is gone, I wonder, I said.

Why? she asked.

Power. There will be a war of power, poverty and everything. I wonder how it will be in the Slums, I said.

Why? she asked.

Where will we hide? We, the slummers of the Slums, those of Mathare, Santa Maria, and those who sleep on the pavements?

Forget it, she said.

We approached a house.

This is the house, she said.

Looks good. You must be having a wonderful time in it. It looks like the house of a mzungu, I said.

We share it. Me and my mate, too bad she is not in, she said.

Who is she? I asked.

Celina. Her mother stays at Eastleigh, she replied.

So she has gone to Eastleigh? I asked.

No. She went to her boy at Ruiru. Chris, a nice chap.

You have things in order, I said.

Yeah. The firm supplies everything. I mean the furniture. The bedding, you have to buy your own.

That is okay, I said.

Let me show you the house. This is our sitting-room, that is the door to Celina's bedroom. This is my bedroom, this is the bathroom with the toilet at the end. This way to the kitchen. This is the kitchen, she showed me.

Women, you are really lucky, I said.

Why? she asked.

In the city people are suffering because there are no houses, while you have a big house here for only the two of you, I said.

150

That is so. But we work here and so accommodation must be supplied, she said.

Well, enjoy your time. But why isn't it fenced like the others? I asked.

I don't know. We found it like that, she said.

Do you have servants too?

No, why? she asked.

The quarters. Who is living there? I asked.

A worker. He works in the firm, she replied.

We kissed and she ran to the kitchen. Light the fire, she told me.

Where is the wood? I asked.

Outside. We have no axe nor a panga, she shouted over. You can use the hoe. It is in the bathroom.

I went out for the logs. Out over the trees the wind blew. The leaves dancing and swaying. What a good waltz, I thought. I carried one big log inside and started hoeing it to pieces. In the kitchen Grace sang 'Come kiss me Love" in a high tone that I smiled at. She must be a nut. I could hear her busy with safurias. She was making the supper. With the rice that she had bought. Eddy, she called out.

Madam, I answered.

How is the fire going? she asked.

Badly, I said.

Why? It is a long time since I did any hoeing, I replied.

Hurry up. The room needs the warmth. It is very cold at night, she said.

I think I will have it burning any time now. How is the cooker? I asked.

Congratulations to a white man. You just turn a knob and it lights up.

With the fire burning I sat on this sofa beside it and had a look at this women's magazine. It had nothing inside except children's and female things. Not for men. Then, Eddy, she called. She must be a monkey, I thought. What was good in my name.

Yeah, I said.

Do you eat fruit at a time like this? she asked.

151

Yes, I said.

Come, then. I went straight to the kitchen and took an orange.

With the supper ready I carried with me this old newspaper with the story about the Beatles getting the MBEs and the old war nuts who had theirs returning them with the protest that the group should not be awarded these medals only for singing and entertaining the royal family. I raised the subject with Grace. The war comrades are right in complaining, I said, showing her the story.

Why are they? she asked.

They deserved their medals for the part they played with death during the wars, I said.

But the group has shown tremendous success in their performance, she said.

It is not the same. Just imagine the bullet and then singing for the Queen. Can you compare them? I don't agree with such awards, I said.

Then tell me, what have you in mind on that subject? she asked.

This is what I have in my mind. The only awards I agree with are the ones obtained in the Olympics. Those medals are okay because everyone is out trying his best to win one. But these given by queens and presidents, never.

But they got them, she said.

Yeah, they did, but only because the Queen perhaps is in love with one of them. Otherwise they wouldn't have got them. There are so many groups in London better than the Beatles, but they have never had them, I said.

You must be a jealous type.

I'm not, I'm only talking facts. If you are on friendly terms with kings, and queens and presidents you will get one. They are all given on friendly terms, I said.

Whatever you say, they got them. I like them and their songs, she said.

But they split up. Each one on his own way, I said.

I used to like that Ringo fellow. He used to smile rarely, she said.

Yeah. Among them all he was my favourite, I said.

From them we switched to the Slums. She demanded to know about the way of living of the waSwahili there. Not so pleasant, I told her. Too corrupt. There is too much begging of salt, curry powder, things like sugar and what ever you are having for your lunch. Most of them are liars and seducers of wives. The women are always admiring young men. Married and single. And the hardship of life in most families. And the production of bastards by young girls as a result of taking sex as a plaything. I always sympathise with those young girls. Nearly all have children. Yeah. All of them. Two, three or four. And with different papas, I said.

My God. Is that how it is? she asked.

Hasn't Sammy told you? I asked.

I never see him and when I see him he is always drunk. I can't ask him.

Then that's how it is. Their lives are all ruined, I said.

But why is it so? she asked.

It is the fault of the parents. They don't care about them. Most of them have no fathers, the mothers are tarts and poor, that is why. They depend on themselves, I said. Too bad, she agreed.

Too bad to you, but they themselves don't see in that way. They never think of the future, I said.

They are used to that life.

That is it. If you removed one of them from there and put him in a place like Ofafa or Jericho, he would prefer death. You would be killing him, I said.

She mentioned Majengo.

That is the name. But it is a good place. You learn a lot from there. It is the oldest of all. The mother of Nairobi. The Old Man stayed there. Obote had a woman there, and so did TJ.

But that boy was good, eh? said Grace.

Very. He was very famous. Before his death he used to come there and talk with the boys, buy them jeans and all that. He liked listening and helping in our troubles. I pity his death. We won't have another boy like him. Never, I said.

He died a premature death, she said.

Yeah. I don't think any death will mean as much as his, I said.

His death split the unity among all the tribes here, she added.

Yeah. It dug a wide gap that will take years and years to close. The harmony of love that was there so that different tribes moved with other tribes, is no longer there. He died with the unity of everything. The people and also the government, I said.

I liked that boy, she said.

Not only you, I said. Everyone.

Forget about him. I feel sleepy, she said. I'm off to bed.

How about the dishes? I asked.

They can wait till tomorrow, she answered.

It was ten o'clock when we woke. With the long boring day still ahead we took a stroll around. We went down towards the station, passing on our way this old and wooden out-of-date police station. Why can't they build an up-to-date police post like those in town? I asked.

I don't know. I'm not in the police force to know that, she answered.

That one at Donholm is the best. You would think it was a state house for police. It has all the coloured decorations and flowers all around. It is very beautiful, the way the stones are laid and the flowers around it, I said.

At the station both young and old were busy selling pork, chicken and fruit to those who were in the train to Nairobi. There was nothing. Nothing interesting, and so we left for the quarters. We could have gone to the factory, but we had no visitor's pass. From the quarters with nothing more to look at we came back to the house. To see anything you must go to Limuru.

After lunch, with nothing to do, we rested on the bed. Fooling about. Then I told her how very high-up women were coming into the Slums to the Sharrifs for black magic over their husbands. And not only them but top men too. Ministers and all.

But why is it so? she asked.

154

How do I know? We only see them coming there daily. Some for love, some for jobs, and others for riches.

But how do they do it for love? I mean the Sharrifs.

That depends. It depends if you are a Muslim. Because there are some times when you have to read and pray at very odd hours. The Sharrifs depend on the Koran. It is in the Koran that all the readings are studied, I explained.

And how about these majini, is it true that they exist? she asked.

I hear that there are some chapters in the Koran which if you read for a time the jini will come to you. I don't know how far that is true. I have even heard that there is a toilet in the Slums there on Kikuyu Street which has a jini. I don't know if it is true.

And do people use the toilet? she asked.

Yeah. They bath in it and shitting too, I said.

Perhaps it is just a rumour of the waSwahili, she said.

Maybe, I said.

It was five when we left the Uplands and took that matatu, worse than a Langata grave, the pirate taxi. The driver kept on adding more passengers without caring. It was a Datsun pick-up. On the way to Limuru we passed six traffic police who never bothered to check for overloading. Instead they only waved at the driver. Corruption, I thought. It is all corruption. At Limuru we took another bus, taking a different route from the one I had come on. It went through Banana. It was Grace's idea so that I could see some parts of Limuru. In my mind I was wondering about her pay. I had snooped while she was in the bath and saw her pay-slip. The woman must be earning a lot. Twelve hundred and single. Shit. She was escorting me up to Banana and then she would take the bus back again. On the route I saw places that I had heard of. Limuru Girls' School, Tigoni hospital, the Youth Centre, Kiambaa, the blanket firm and this Matiba flower place and all. At Banana she got off, promising to see me next weekend when she drops in town. Going on, I envied the coffee plantations and maize at Gachie. Around Muthaiga, the diplomats' mansions. At Parklands, the Aga Khan hospital. This nut must be a thief. He owns so many things and is the leader of the Ismailis. He has no

155

country and has just married somebody's wife. Not even an Ismaili. I laughed at that thought. A leader with no country. And the nuts he was leading are just scattered all over the world. And him living in France. The city of life and prostitutes. Shit, the leader and his followers. His followers can even lick his spit praying to wake up the next morning rich like him.

At Brilliant I thought of Zakia. I smiled. I wondered what she was doing now. Perhaps she was looking for me. Or at the Sharrif's. Crazy women. Back at Machakos Airport I dropped off and headed straight for the Slums. I wanted it. It was a long time since that of yesterday afternoon. The dope. At Katanga it was hard to trace Hussein. He was not around. Looking for the dope from Ruri I found nothing. His mate Musumar was not around. Kadugunye too had nothing. At Sophy too. We then took to Eastleigh. Me, Jabbir, Buddy Guy, Zablon, Mwachi and Issa. From this nut we got some rolls. We then left for Ziwani. There we got it. Back to California we went to this house at the top of the fourth stair. We rolled the whole of it and dopped it off. From there we took to Rash's kiosk. With the mbaazi in my stomach and the full glass on top of it I retired to the car. Hussein was not there. I slept.

6

Monday morning the news spread of Rimaka and the Arab. The
Dog Section police got them red-handed last night in an alley. Shit,
this Rimaka. Of all the homos. That started the cursing by the
boys. It's the Arabs' game, commented Burma. So it is nothing
new. Yossa wished that it were on one of the rap rap of the slums.
Girls, I said. Omari thought of history. He cursed most of all Julius
Caesar. He was a man for all the women and a woman for his
soldiers. He cursed da Vinci and Aristotle. Jabbir wished that what
was done to the Arabs in Zanzibar by that Field Marshal should
happen to them everywhere. It is why the Israelis are beating them.
They think of nothing else but the act. I told them that that
Hiroshima bomb ought to be dropped now. It was a mistake in the
year they dropped it. It is now that the world is evil. There is no
need of living, I said. The curses about Rimaka were interrupted
by the announcement of the shooting of the Apollo 14 to the moon.
It raised an argument between Omari and Suleiman. Omari
favoured the Russians, Suleiman the Americans. The Russians
send theirs without astronauts while the Americans must send
their Apollo with astronauts in it, said Omari. We all favoured the
Russians and Suleiman got annoyed. He was prepared to fight
Omari. Then came the bow-legged Magambo. A boy with a sharp
mouth, and funny. He mocked Suleiman, telling him that wise
men of today don't fight. If you want to fight, join the army. But
too bad for you. You can't run or shoot in the range. You are very
unfit, he mocked. We laughed at that. He had fixed Suleiman.
Then it was his turn to get fixed. In his bottom pocket was a yellow
card. The card known by all. It can only be got from the STC, that
VD clinic. The boys told him that he was burning. He defended

himself, that that was a certificate. A playboy has to have it. That ended it. He tore the card up. The boredom remained.

I was in my new outfit and going from Yasmin hotel feeling very satisfied when I told Hussein where I was going to. My washing rags were with Ocham. He had to wash them and keep them safe for me, together with the other pair. I was on my way through Bondeni when I passed this Wamboi woman at the Mfereji wa Dhambi. She looked down and avoided me. To hell with you. If you are expecting me to come to you, too bad. She whispered something I thought odd about me to her friends. Among them Wanjiku, Irene, her sister Wangoi, the short-foot Njeri and this ass Wambue. They all looked at me. Shit, I cursed them. Perhaps she was telling them how I'd forgotten her. Shit, I cursed them again. What are you? You are killers. Aborters. Who will marry you? God bless you all.

I moved fast again when I met with this Mumbi. I said hello and told her to say hello to her boy Obadiah. A nut. I took the path behind to avoid seeing the parked family buses. The carvers were busy carving the handcrafts for sale to tourists in the evening in town. Some for export. I passed these slums and kiosks with late lunchers eating lunch. Near the bridge I met this Mamu of Gorofani. She was pregnant. My God. The second one. She was not even eighteen yet. God. When will these Slums girls realise that Africa and the whole world is in a critical condition where no more births are needed? When will they realise that Africa is corrupt and living under a reign of fear? Black leaders who would even turn to a white thief for advice because that nut is white? I wished they knew what I had in my mind every day. That the black man was not yet ready to rule himself because of poverty. The freedom they were fighting for was nothing but death and corruption. Coups, too. For seekers of power and riches. You will hear them blurting out about liberation in Rhodesia, Angola, Mozambique and Guinea Bissau, but taking no action to encourage the freedom fighters. Listen to them in UN and OAU. They blast it all through their mouths of what the white man ought to do. Why should he, the same white man, while he still wants to enjoy himself? Listen to them begging the guy. Listen how they were pleading with the white man to stop the massacre of the blacks in Mozambique. Hear them in the UN. After all, the UN is for them, the rich aristocratic nations. The world powers. Hear them in the OAU meetings, condemning the evils of the white man. How will that help to free the ones they want liberated? It only increases the thirst of the Portuguese to kill before they leave, making history for themselves like that My Lai fellow Cally in Viet Nam. I always denounced this organisation. I thought it was only a good platform for the black aristocratic nations, where the intellectuals in their new fashions of black suits and their Oxford English talk without looking at the scripts written for them. That was OAU. It helped no common man. A slum man knew nothing about it. It was an organisation of black mafias. A gangsters' club. Watch what they were doing themselves in their own countries. See the firing of thieves in Nigeria, the clubbing, the firing squads for suspected guerrillas. All tied on stakes. Is that what they called Liberation? Was that the result of hard-won uhuru? No. It was a reign of terror. A reign of fear and terror. The terror of black man over black man. It was fear. Will it succeed? This liberation? Why not the Russians' style? Invasion. Invade Rhodesia, Angola, Mozambique and Guinea Bissau like the Russians did Czechoslovakia. That was the true politics. True politics comes from the barrel of a gun. And it should be done by all the African countries. Unite. You have the planes which were given to you, and those you bought. Invade them. That is true politics. Do that, beat the Boers in South Africa, and that way the real meaning of the OAU will be seen. Forget about sharing a table with them. You commit yourselves so much. You commit yourselves because when signing for that aid, you promised never to touch any white man. And in that way, you were told, anything, any aid will be granted. Loans. But with strings tied. That way you were not free. You had no uhuru. I think uhuru is self-reliance, when you don't turn to a neighbour for security, money and advice. If you were poor, remain poor. That way you were used to it, to what you have got. And that was why I always adored the socialism of Mwalimu Nyerere. He was really a mwalimu. I thought of all these things at the sight of this Mamu on my way to town for a movie. I wanted to be far from the Slums.

It was Tuesday morning, seated by this skeleton of a Renault car and talking about the crowd at the Chief's camp, when Brazze came up.

What is that long line for? he pointed towards that direction.

Perhaps they wanted to join the National Service, said Yossa.

No, they want to register for land, answered Burma. There will be some land distribution in the River Valley.

They must be crazy, said Mayanja. A jobless with no money to develop the land wanting land. He spat.

A mistake, said Burma. It is a mistake that will one day be regretted.

What mistake? asked Kesho, who was never at all attentive.

The distribution of land. These leaders must be cheating us, said Burma.

It is a way of campaigning for re-election, said Zablon.

This time I won't vote, cursed Burma. We all supported that. The chap I could vote for is no longer there.

Yeah, we all agreed. The death of politics stole him from us, said Mayanja.

But why don't we slummers elect someone from here instead of voting for these people whom we don't even know where they come from? asked Yossa.

You wouldn't have a chance, said Bez.

Why not? asked Kesho.

You have no money to buy the votes and the people, answered Bez.

No one will vote for you, said Hussein.

That is it, I said. That is the whole problem with waSwahili. They all think they know everything. If a guy like you stands they will start wanting to know what you have to offer them.

Yeah, supported all.

They are very poor men, said Burma. They think that they know a lot, yet they know nothing. See how backward they are!

They never advance, said Yossa.

160

You will still see them taking their children to learn the Koran. In this century who needs to read the Koran? People are learning geography, maths and English while others read the Koran, Burma said.

We roared with laughter.

Mahibilisi, abused Yossa. To hell with politics too. It is a dangerous game.

That is so, I commented. When you are in it your life is dangling at the end of a loose pendulum.

It is either detention or death, said Burma.

Yeah, men, and too bad if two friends are fighting for the same thing, said Bez. One must rot in detention while the other is sipping wine.

Politics is all shit, said Mayanja. Did you see the leader of the opposition party, that Ja-Nam, when he came out?

He was down to the bones, said Yossa.

Take a look at that one of Zambia too, added Hussein.

Yeah, that bearded Kapwepwe and Kaunda, added Kesho. Kapwepwe is now rotting in prison.

I told you, I said. The whole of Africa has nothing but corrupt cowards.

Yeah, man, supported all.

And have a look at a guy like Boneko, said Burma. He has been there the whole of his political life.

It is all shit, repeated Mayanja.

Too bad, with African countries, said Yossa. The peasants have no voice to criticise like those in London and America.

And still they claim to be independent, added Bez.

And democratic too, said Burma.

Things will change one day and it will be too bad for them, said Kesho.

The topic got cut off when these women from Bondeni passed us. They were Wango, Njiko, Mbui and Wamaitha. Also Irene, who was the youngest and more beautiful than the rest. We all admired her and talked of how each of us would love her.

But how long will they last? asked Burma. How long will they be like that with all the boogies, the day-time dances in town?

Give them a year and then look at them, said Jabbir, who had joined the party. You won't like any part of her, said Mayanja. Who wants Ritah now? Nobody, said Hussein. She is all worn out.

And then think of her at the time when Idaho could kill someone for her sake, said Jabbir.

Let them die, if that is what they want, cursed Burma.

They are all shit, added Mayanja. Moving toilets.

Nowadays they want us instead of us wanting them, said Bez.

Their days are gone, said Kesho. They better look for old pensioners.

Who will take them? asked Mayanja. Those slobs have swung with them.

Too bad for the women of today, said Zablon.

Then Kadugunye joined us. He asked me about the movie.

Very boring, I said. Good only for lawyers.

Those women came in yesterday just after you had left, he said.

What did they say? I asked.

Zakia said she would come back, he said.

That is another task again, I said. Perhaps things went bad at Sharrif's.

Women, cursed the boys. Listen to what they are doing to men, said Bez.

And Wamboi too wants to see you, said Hussein. She wants to know why you are avoiding her.

To hell. She is a schoolgirl.

Women, women, women, said Mayanja. Shit.

Yeah, liberation soldiers, added Kesho.

They want equality with men, said Yossa.

Then the mwathini bellowed. We all took to crumbs at the mosque and dispersed in twos and threes. Some went for the addition of more miraa. We bought ours too, and walked around the Slums, passing some people at a funeral playing the gramophone and dancing and drinking. We thought that when someone dies most of the people must be happy. We walked and walked till late at night, when we took the ten-cents coffee and retired to our wrecks of homes.

In the morning, with all of us at this skeleton of a Renault, lazing in the morning sunshine, came these City inspectors. With them, senior officers in the City Hall and the County Council. We smelt something fishy. Some stinking odour. They moved around the scraps of our homes. We watched them with curiosity. They had also been to Santa Maria. With them also was a health inspector. And to guard them were the City askaris with batons. As we were still wondering about them, along came another dark blue Benz with the flag of the City mayor dancing on it. Out of it came the mayor. Following her the two councillors of the Slums, Dolli and Muthee. Dolli, a woman. And one of the Councillors. We watched them. The time had come. It was now going to be true. The demolition of the Slums. Recently they had removed all the landlords to the new flats with those of their tenants who could afford the rents of the new buildings. The maskinis, the poor, remained in the old mud houses with brown rusted roofs. Not only the poor, but among them some highly paid and well earning nuts. Also those who had trained in communist nations. A nut like Musa who was a major in the Chinese army. And Elijah too. The nut who was one of the gang whose coup was foiled. They all could be found in the Slums. So the visitors inspected the wrecks. Burma wanted to know from Dolli what the hell it was all about but she avoided him. She sensed what questions she would have to answer from the boys. Then one of the visitors said it. *Hapa mahali pa wakora. Watoto ya shilingi mbili.* That entered and cut our hearts into two. That our wrecks were hide-outs for crooks and that we were children of two shillings. He was lucky there were the askaris. He would have known better, that we were not there because we liked being there but because of taabu. Troubles. We will start with that one at Digo, said the mayor, and then pull down the rest. After Digo (meaning the Santa Maria village), will follow the towing away of these wrecks here. Our homes. That ended all our hope. All hope of living and all our time. The plan was on the way. At first it didn't sound as if they meant it but now it was true. The

Slums must come down. It was the part of the City Council's plan for new houses. Damn the City. Where will they take all the slummers? That was it, Kariobangi. They will all be dumped into Kariobangi. But that was for those who were working. How about the mothers, the viruka njias, their bastards and all of us? Having decided what they were going to do, they all left. We talked about this and that, cursing the mayor, the lot of them, everyone. Asked Burma: Where does the government want us to go? Said Jabbir: It is their idea, those whom we elected. They were the government, not us. Remained the question, when will they do it? That was the question that spread everywhere in the Slums. Some blamed the two councillors. Why didn't they tell us? But it had been said before and spread all over the newspapers. Let them do what they want to do. We won't die because of that. One day we shall overcome, remarked Burma.

Then as we were still thinking about the visitors and what they had said, came this noise from the direction of the mosque. It was mixed with laughter and followed with stone-throwing. The taxi-men enjoyed the fun while the gate-sitters at the mosque waved and hit out with their walking-sticks, In the confusion Ambari's turban fell off, leaving his grey hair to be seen. The mob was all watching now and those who were waiting for the bus turned around to watch. Cochio and Kulumbu kept on laughing their heads off. We ran to see what the whole comedy was about. Ah. Shit. Bullshit. So it was only them. A lady dog and a gentleman. Dogs. Shit. Man! What a beating these innocent creatures of dogs were getting. What a brutality. Where were the KSPCA? This scene needed them. Damn them. The stoning went on. Most of the stoners being Muslims. Hunger must be in charge of them. They were merciless. Too bad for the dogs to have chosen to display themselves near the mosque and at a time like this of fasting. Man, if those animals could talk I don't know what they would have said. Nothing, I thought. We forgot about the City Council men.

We went back and nothing was talked about except this scene. The whole of Katanga Base had only that in mind. The fasting women didn't want to see the scene. At first they thought that it

164

was something good for them. On seeing it, they pulled the buibuis over the bridge of their noses to hide their laughter. First they spat. They pretended to hate the dogs while perhaps in fact not doing so. Some it reminded of the game, bringing the whole picture into their eyes and brains. They were happy but because men were around they couldn't show it. If there had been no men they would have died laughing.

In the afternoon the accident occurred. It was due to the negligence of Njoroge. They were washing the SBS bus and on top, doing the roof, was Mura. Njoroge was in the bus fooling with the starter, started the engine and set free the hand-brake. It rolled ahead. Mura, who knew nothing of what was happening, when we shouted and Njoroge applied the brakes came tumbling down, rolling over the windscreen to the ground. On his head banged his debe, splashing all the water on his head. Perhaps it was this water that cured him. We called Njoroge all the evil names living in our brains. We cursed him so much that it was lucky that curses can't kill or break any bones. He stood dumb. We inspected Mura for any fracture. He had none. But perhaps he was hurt internally. We never attended hospitals unless for something very serious. Our hospital was the one near the bridge. The special treatment clinic.

In the evening, just before the bellowing of mwathini, two dead corpses were carried to the Muslims' cemetery in Kariokor. The Makaburini. They must have eaten enough during their time on earth. What a good month to die, I thought, when people were thinking and fasting falsely to Mohammed, the prophet and Allah the boss. They will sit next to him, near his chair. Then I thought of death. At times like this I always thought of death. That darkness in the coffin under the ground and how you will never come out again. How you will remain forever in there with ants tickling you, making you laugh with all the bare teeth out as a sign of burning down there. What a good picture your skeleton made.

At Masadukuni at night, that evening, we met Rash, Adija, Nuru, Fatuma, her sister Zuena, Farida, Susy, Njambi and Kasa. All young mothers of the Slums and aborters. They were out to get money for their young ones' milk. With them some old mamas who were after young blood to push them. All clad in buibuis. With them too were Josse, Mwaura, Dan, Franco, Saidi, Burma who was after Sera, Wangare after Dan. Then Rash threw her request to me with a nickname, I don't know where she got it from. She needed a bottle. Will you take cham? It is cheaper and quick in stimulation, I said. Where is it? she asked.

Say yes or no, will you take it? I asked.

Yes, she agreed.

Then let's go. Accompanying us were Susy, Fatuma, Wangare and Burma. We headed for Mama Atieno's. That one would kill them in no time, we knew that. It was very powerful. On our way we blew the last rolls of gabba. At Mama Atieno's the order began. A full glass each for the women. They gulped them down. We paid and left, ready for the reactions to form in them. This was the big idea behind it. We took our way to Katanga in case they couldn't manage the walk. It was a quick walk, otherwise they wouldn't reach it. Behind the fence of Ukumbusho, Susy shitted. At Katanga I took Rash to our car. She was out. The stuff had had a quick reaction on her. Hussein brought in Fatuma. She too was out. Burma took Wangare to the Pontiac, whose owner was serving a seven-year term for forgery. I thought how surprised he would be when he came out and found the condition of his American pride. I wondered if Kibibi would let him in with nothing in his pocket. Lucky for Odongo, he was not at Masandukuni. He took Susy who was now being a nuisance, begging for a sleep.

It was Saturday morning. I kept on thinking of this scattered family of ours. In the afternoon I must go to Kariobangi to try and trace Atiesh. She eloped there with a crook and now she was in the business of selling cham. I must find her. Tandra is okay with Dommy who had joined the Prison Corps. I have some friends there who might know her whereabouts. Thuos and Ngangas are there with their mother and their sister Karuras and Wanjikos. They might know. As I was thinking about that, in rolled the car of this woman, Zakia. The Alfa Romeo. I approached her and we

166

talked all about last week, how she had come and missed me, me giving out the reasons and so on. Then she laid it on me. What the Sharrif did and how what he had promised her would happen when the work was done didn't work out. Then, don't you know any other one? she asked. Let's try that one at California. That Issa Kamchape. He might try it for you, I said. We drove there. On the way she told me how deceitful she suspected the Sharrif to be.

At Issa's I introduced her to him. I then explained everything to him and left them to carry on with the work. I told the lady that she would meet me at Katanga. I left. On my way I met this nut of a Moffat in the mob. The mob who preached the gospel of Jesus. Of all the people, this Moffat. I stood and listened to him preaching how evil he was, how he was a son lost in sin. How he drank, whored about with pros and so on. I couldn't believe it. Of all the boys Moffat to be saved from sin by Jesus. A good absorber like Moffat. I listened to his preaching. We then happened to look at each other in the face. He tried to hide it but I was fast enough. I winked at him. He stumbled and got confused in what he was talking about. Then followed the music. He played the maracas. God must have been a musician, I thought. A guitar, a microphone, maracas and an accordion. The musicians were both ladies and men. They shouted, but nobody paid much attention to what they were preaching about. That is the mistake of the black man. He can never support a fellow black man's religion. But watch him at Kamukunji when the Vietnam killers come there. The Americans. And with them organs, microphones and a bass guitar and speakers. And then their uniforms. Like that Ken Foreman and his family who came along there with the same lies as those other two, Oral Roberts and Morello, saying that they could heal and make cripples walk, the blind see and all that shit. The Americans! Cheats and liars. Imagine a family preaching the words of Jesus and making false promises of healing the sick. And then to fool us the more they brought with them a black negro woman to sing her gospel blues, the same like those in the boogies. I always remember that Carol with the Foreman family. They were no different from the Beatles. Only in the uniform. They had on black suits with funny ties. It was not even like a preaching rally. It was modelling. A fashion show. Then the black nut of a preacher who also tried to fool us by the cream Crimplene suit he had on. That pastor James of Kariokor. He kept on adjusting his tie and putting on and removing his sunglasses. Damn preachers and black pastors. Thinking of that I left the mob. Shit of Moffat. He was one of us. That bow-legged nut, a good friend of Karuku. I wondered where the hell Karuku was.

Back at Katanga we managed two cars, a kombi and a new 504, before the Zakia woman came to life. I did her car too. She paid me a pound for it. She roared away. I told Hussein where I had taken her. Their problems, he remarked.

In the afternoon, forgetting about going to Kariobangi, we drank and found ourselves at Camay in the boogy. On the stage were Kangees and the Hodis. It was full. We danced in twos and sometimes with the local tarts. Then we thought of having a revenge on the bottle-pickers. We must punish them by making them drink our urine. Nearing break time we took ourselves to the toilets with our half finished bottles and filled them to the necks. We went back and put them on the tables, and stood aside to watch them picked. At break time they were all picked. And we saw the pickers absorbing them with no care. The one who took Burma's offered a sip to a girl. That was it. They drank the urine full of VD viruses. Burma got the disease on the night we took them in the cars. Wangare infected him. We left and took to Acadia. With the same idea of punishment. At Acadia there was a fight. This slummer Rajab and this Olympic silver medallist boxer Dick. We watched them. No one tried to separate them. We knew why. Rajab was a jealous nut. He was the leader of the Sun Valley gang. They fought like bulls. Head butt and fists. Finally they separated, and we booked in. While the Glorias played we took the bottles down to the toilet on the stairs and filled them. On the tables we watched them picked. Too bad. My God, too bad. One of them was this woman like an American from Shauri Moyo, Jacinta. She picked Burma's bottle. My God, who will get a kiss from that tart, we thought. We then thought of Starlight. Lucky for them. They never played on Saturday afternoons. We wished it was a Sunday.

Jemima would have drunk it. She was always there. But funny. She never grew old. That skinny bent-foot of a woman. When the boogy ended the gang fight started. Sun Valley against Sicheki. It was over women. The Sun Valleys wanted to hijack girls.

It was Sunday morning while we were all seated here on this damn skeleton of a Renault when this Peter fellow surprised me. It was three years since I saw him. We were together in the same band during my time in music when I was still in school. After our separation he had joined the Superphonics and they went to Nakuru. From Nakuru they left for Kampala. He wrote me only once telling me that they had joined and signed a contract in Grand Hotel. He surprised me because the coup found him there and I never expected to see him. Hearing the news of the coup I had thought first of him and his wife. And now he was here. A surprise to me. Hello, hello man, I said. Is it really you or is it you? I began.

It is me and the same me, he replied.

I can't believe it. I thought you were in the group of men murdered as guerrillas, I said.

No, I was not, he replied. The boys listened to him.

And how was it? asked Burma.

No joke, it was murder. They murdered those men for nothing, he said.

You mean that they were not guerrillas? asked Mayanja.

No, they were just suspects and got it, he answered.

And how was it that day? asked Bez.

You could think that it was a miracle day. People climbed trees and squeezed together to watch the condemned men shot. We were awoken in the very early hours of morning when the soldiers were having a check on guerrillas. And then we were forced to go and watch. It was terrible, he explained.

How about that boy? Was he too a guerrilla? asked Urai.

No. The thing is, he was found in the house of the suspected men, he said.

How about the expulsion of the Asians? Suleiman asked.

They refused Daddy's demands. You see, when that millionaire

Madhvani died, he left so many properties and buildings. So what Daddy wanted was to be the sole proprietor of the whole Madhvani group. The Asians refused. He even wanted to have Madhvani's wife. So, when the Asians refused, he got vexed. Going to the bank to have a check on the account, he found only thirteen shillings and fifty cents. That put the Asians in the hot pot. Going back to them, they offered him two million shillings to leave them alone. He refused. He left them assuring them that they were in the hot soup. And like the Israelis who were ordered out because Meir refused to give him a Phantom jet to blow Tanzania with, and the ten million he wanted, they got ninety days to pack out. That began the great Asian Exodus, he explained.

And we heard that many of them committed suicide, is it true? asked Juma.

Yeah. Many did. Those who were very rich, with big cars. I think you know the pride of the Asians with their big cars. They were selling them cheaply. The buildings and the businesses. So what most of them did with their cars, they put salt in the petrol tanks. So when you bought it, perhaps a Benz, after a short journey the engine burst, he said.

But that was okay, I said. These whites, especially Asians, are very proud and yet in India they are dying like small poked chicken. They are really milkers, I added.

Any white, supported Burma. They are all the same. Nothing but milkers.

I wish we got one like that Daddy fellow, said I, but who is not a killer like him. Someone to chase out the proud Asians. A guy like Lumumba.

Or Karume, said Brazze. Marry them by force or kick them out.

That nut was a seaman, said Suleiman. And I think you know how seamen are. He set an example by having two of the Persian beauties. We laughed.

But that made history for himself, said Omari. The world won't forget him. More uproar of laughter.

Yeah, man, supported Burma. And that is how the black leaders should be. If they were all like that, there wouldn't have been such long delays and struggles for the freedom fighters.

They would have united and invaded South Africa, Angola, Guinea Bissau and Mozambique and the whole thing would have been okay, said Mayanja.

But they are afraid, said Abu.

They mind too much about their businesses and possessions, said Bez.

They think of nothing but how to get rich quickly, added Omari.

When Peter left we talked a little of Uganda and the disappearance of top important people. We concluded that Daddy too was a coward.

In the afternoon according to yesterday's plan, I rolled to Shauri Moyo to board a matatu, private taxi, for Kariobangi. At Shauri Moyo at this corner near the Burma market, sitting on a stone, were the crippled Anne, Temmy, Mary and Lucie, all mothers. I spat because of how they bullshitted me. They whispered something odd about me. They all looked at me. Temmy looked aside. Shit, I cursed her. Why didn't your Singh of your boyfriend marry you?

At the gate of Burma, Kiroko was busy shoe-shining and so was Wango. The gamblers went on with their shouts of *Wekelea*. Put money, get money, they bellowed. I bought a roll from Irungu and left Oronge shouting and calling me names. The maize roasters laughed out stupidly. A fool is born a fool, I said to myself. Oronge the Refuse Vehicle nut was a fool.

At the stage I didn't take long to wait. It then came, this old bending-on-one-side Morris. Its springs worn out due to overloading. I hopped in and squeezed between the passengers. Man! This van was worse than a grave. Worse than those drawers in the mortuary with the deads in them. And worse than those graves at Langata cemetery. Worse because you were travelling at your own risk. There were the traffic police and accidents. The van was meant for eight only. We were over twenty in it and at each stop one passenger was added. I was in it with my heart in my hands. Fear of traffic police and of an accident. For a traffic policeman it would be a hell of a chase around the estate and the locations. These drivers never stopped unless chased by the motor-bike fellows. And when caught, it was always money speaking to square it. We left behind Kaloleni, Makongeni, Bahati, Mbotela, Ofafa, then at the corner entering Makadara, seated on his motor bike, was an officer of the traffic police. My heart skipped several beats. We were all for it. Everyone stopped breathing. We held our mouths tight on the hard benches of our seats. Even if you wanted to give out a fart it disappeared. It sensed danger too. Our driver, Macharia, who was a slummer but a nut with eyes for money, who had escaped our daily laziness at Katanga and got himself a matatu on the routes of Kariobangi, looked calm. He took a corner and headed straight towards Jericho. Expecting the officer behind us I looked at the back window to see him coming. But . . . he was just where he was. Not even looking at the tortured van with all our weights. Then Macharia explained it all. It is money nowadays, he said. Who does not need it? He gave out a laugh. I knew what you all were expecting. Never worry when you are in my van. I know them all and they too know me. That Maina knows me. We always meet in the evening at that Maro Bar, he finished.

That was it, I thought. The Americans call it the Dollar. That is why they want to dominate the world by building bases anywhere, far from their homes. And so do the French and other world powers in the United Nations. It is why the French are testing their H-bombs. Shit. And all in the Dark Man's Continent. And what does a black man do? He cries at the Commonwealth white-man club. And at the same time the Portuguese are sticking their bayonets in the hearts of black freedom fighters. To hell with liberation movements. I love them. You fight and die and then in the end a non-fighter who was hiding in London with the whores there comes and takes the leadership. Damn them all. If you get a white tear him up. Eat them as Lumumba said to his Congolese. That was the national hero, Patrice Lumumba.

Entering Rabai Road and the new estates of Uhuru, Harambee and heading towards Outer Ring we passed another policeman who was only waving us through. That brought another remark. That is Onyango, said Macharia. If he stops me I just hand out my licence and a pound in it. No more trouble. He chuckled as he accelerated more. Leaving behind the SOS and not entering the South we entered Kariobangi. At the church I hopped out and headed to this place, Maskani as they called it. Thuo and Nganga's place. At home they were not in. I headed to their mother's place. I found the mother busy making tea. At first she couldn't recognise me. Then she brought my face to her memory. Wooi, wooi, she remarked. So it is you?

Yes. It is me, I said.

You are old. You were very young at the time we left Mbotela, she said, looking at me all over but most at my beard and sideburns.

I said nothing but smiled.

How are the others? she asked

That is it, I thought. She does not know that they died, mother and father. She does not know that we are all scattered. Then I laid it all before her. She couldn't believe it. I told her how scattered we were. She sympathised with me. She then told me that Ngotho, the father, died two years after we left Mbotela. I told her that Thuo told me that one day when we met in a boogy. She told me that Karanjas the elder son was in London doing brewery training, Maggwa was an accountant in Thika, Ngangas was doing a course with the CID on finger printing, Thuos had joined the brewery people, Wanjikos was doing Form Three and the other two boys were still in primary school. That was Shombas and Mainas.

How about Karuras? I asked.

That one is a nut. A hard-headed woman. She depends on her own self, she said.

Is she working? I asked.

No, we put her to commercial studies, to do shorthand and typing, but she thought of marriage. But that didn't get her anywhere. She is now a tramp, she said. I noticed that she was vexed.

Too bad, I said. And where are they now? Thuos and Ngangas?

At the hall, she said. Doing this, and she made a fist-punch.

Oh, thank you, I said. Let me see them. I left for the hall. I found them practising some shadow boxing and sparring. Thuos recognised me first. Hello, Eddy, damn you. Where are you hiding? he asked.

Down there, man. In the Slums. Then they all came, forgetting their practising. Then followed the introductions; this is Dick, the nut who represented us recently in the East African boxing in Kampala. This one is Felix, who came from Munich in the Olympics, introduced Thuos.

Is he the one called Maina? I asked.

That is it, they all agreed.

And why don't the City Council give you a nice hall if the Slums can produce boxers like these for such occasions? I asked.

We don't know, perhaps they don't recognise the Slums, answered Dick.

This hall is no worse than those toilets of Kaloleni and Ziwani, I remarked. They will think of it one day.

Then the introductions went on. This is Keffa, this is Nyota and others whose names I couldn't hold in my skull. We then left for their Maskani. There we planned our boozing. I was a guest of honour. The drink was the smuggled one from Uganda, the triple times distilled waragi. They called it ching. Thuos left for it. We waited and talked of this and that. Then both Dick and Felix wanted to know if I had been a boxer before. Yeah, I said and Ngangas supported me. He was a tough nut a bantamweight, said Ngangas. He looks like one, said Dick. Then Thuos came in with the bottle nicely wrapped. We drank it with them diluting theirs. I took mine dry. They couldn't believe their eyes to see me taking mine dry. Then we left for more from their stores. No difference from those in the Slums. They have no names. Only the nicknames, like ours. We popped into the mud houses, gulping a shilling each. Then we came back to Maskani to have in our tummies a roasted kilo of meat. Passing the door to the other room, their bedroom, on the way to the toilet, I didn't notice this woman on the bed. Coming back I saw her. Her face to the wall. I didn't make any comments. I knew I would be a nuisance if I started. Back to the gang. I stood at the window looking out. The others had their private talk. My mind came to rest on this cat resting peacefully on this drawer. I looked at its ear, the left one, which was on my side. Then a silly idea came into my mind, I didn't know why. An evil idea. A killing idea. Looking at its ear I thought, suppose I held it, stroking its fur, and then tied its paws, stuck a fire-cracker or an explosive in the cavity and set fire to it, what a surprise the cat would have. That idea got shattered when this Blastus came in. I knew the name after they called him. He offered us a round. We left and headed for this Muratina bar. With enough in me, I shared a bottle with Thuos. Sitting in a corner, my eyes through this small window rested on the drinkers on the other side. Men. Between them only one woman. I started counting the men. Eleven in all. I thought what a story the woman could tell if they all raped her in there.

Then, still in that bar, in came Pocomoco, Burma, Kaffod, Brazze, Bez, Mayanja, Omari, Odongo, Jabbir, Zablon, Baker the international driver and Suleiman. They all came in one kombi. Finding me there they were surprised. How did you come here, man? they asked.

By a matatu, I said.

Then Brazze said it. Where can we get that cham, the Uganda waragi? We hear it is around this place.

That is no worry, I said. I'm with them. The members of the thing. I indicated to them the Thuos gang.

We need some, said Burma. How much do they sell a bottle for?

Seventeen shillings, said Thuos. But that is to us. As for yourselves, if you go there they won't sell it.

Then why don't you go and buy it for us? uttered Kaffod.

Sure, Jabbir added. Go and bring us some.

How many bottles do you want? asked Thuos.

Enough for all of us. Let's all contribute and buy enough bottles.

That is it, said Kaffod. Let's do just that. We had had enough so we exempted ourselves from the contribution. Their contribution brought them three bottles. They drank. Finishing it up we got into that kombi, from an Embassy where Baker had got a job, with his international licence. The Thuos gang stayed behind because it would be a hell of a time for them to come back. And that was after Kaffod had started blasting out his usual feelings when drunk on the domination of things by one tribe in the whole country. That is how he was any time when he was drunk. Always against the government.

We took the Eastleigh route. At Eastleigh we branched and headed straight to the roundabout. At the roundabout we went straight to Section Three. At Fourteenth Street we turned left. It was Burma's idea because a new bridge had been built connecting Eastleigh and Kimathi Estate. In the bush of grass, still standing, was the paper house of Mwangi and family. A sign stood on the fence. At the bridge we stopped to piss into the river. Then at Jerusalem we met and passed this nut with Mau Mau-like hair. We booed at him. On his face were black sunglasses. Half of his head was bald. He looked like a Luo. We then took the Heshima Road, heading back to the Slums, passing on our way the never-used ticket cubes. Some firms have money to waste, we thought. At Virginia's kiosk, she was busy with her young child on her back preparing the evening meal. Then Baker got wild at the wheel. And all due to Burma's encouragement. Come on, he urged him. Step on the gas. He sent it roaring in top gear, taking sharp corners, torturing the tyres. We shouted. Then we headed for it. Taking the corner of both Shauri Moyo at Burma and the one at the Seventh Day church.

I can't remember how it was, or who caused it, or anything. The van went out of control and when we came to be aware of what was happening, it had missed the road and was heading straight for the river. Though Baker tried to control the steering, it just swung in a circle. With the last sight of this bridge (as to when was it built, that was 1938) I remembered no more. We plunged in.

I had been in this private ward in the hospital in ward eleven where I was pushed on this bed out to bed number five. I could see and hear but I had no memory of anything. I didn't know how I had been shitting or pissing or even if I had shitted at all. I didn't know if I had even eaten anything since I came in. With the morning sun out I managed a stroll and went out to sit on the grass. I was after

176

some sun bathing. On the grass I made friends with a Shifta boy. He was a victim of the Shifta war. His parents had been killed in the war over a border clash. His name was Aden. He had been in the hospital for the last five years. He came here after he was saved by the troops with a wound in his back. He was only five years old at that time. Having no family or relative or anyone to take care of him, he was now a government body. He was the only friend I had here. After lunch we came out again. Then with an hour to go before the visitors' hour we were back on our beds waiting for the fathers, mothers, brothers, sisters, relatives and friends. I watched the visitors entering our ward for anyone I knew. There was no one. They came near my bed to others while I watched. I knew no one among the lot. The pain of loneliness speared my heart. I felt like committing suicide.

For three days that procedure took place, watching them come in and going. That doubled my heartache. No one for me. Not even a slummer. Only Aden, who would come and keep me busy with his talk. He was used to it, he would explain, and laugh, asking me if I was like him. Then the fourth night it happened. The man on bed six died and so did the one on bed four. That scared me to death. But I wished after they were replaced that it had been me. I would have no more troubles.

The next day came my surprise. From ward twenty-two came Walker, to bed six. A relief at least to be with a slummer. In the morning sun we talked about the Slums. Then a bomb fell on me. He told me that only two are alive: Pocomoco and Burma. Burma lost a foot and Pocomoco came round the day after the accident. You are very lucky, you three, he said. He then went on, they have started pulling down the Slums. Rash and her friends told me.

Do they come here?

Yes. Every evening. Only today they will not know where I have been transferred to.

That was it. Another mortar into my Viet Nam body and soul. I didn't want to hear more. In the evening they came. Rash, Sophia, Fatuma, Mary, Amina, Nuru, Sera and Adija. They told me the same thing. Walker told me. All the Slums of Santa Maria were no longer there. The place had been fenced by the Air Force people. The Kajificheni, Sun-Valley Square, Santa Maria and the plots, that of Wagunya and the one of the Borans, were no more. The City Council brought in a bulldozer to demolish everything. Two days later Walker kicked the bucket. It was at night, and in the morning you would have thought that he was only sleeping. I cried. Why not me too? Why Walker, and not the rich slobs? Why Walker, just a slummer who has nothing, a poor son of a poor man, a boy who has enjoyed nothing? Why not Nixon, Kissinger, Caetano, Smith, Vorster, why not all the whites? Why not everyone? Why not me? And why not the whole wide world? And the Pope? Damn death. Damn the whole world and living. And damn Jesus too. Why is anyone living? Why is the black man living? Why is he living under nothing but fear, terror, torture and death? I wish I knew about that Hiroshima bomb, now I would liberate the whole world. I would liberate Angola, Guinea Bissau, Mozambique, Viet Nam, Cambodia, I would liberate the Americans from Nixon, Spiro Agnew and Kissinger, I would liberate the Irelanders from the Queen's troops, the Arabs from Israel, leave the Chinese in peace, liberate the whole world with the Hiroshima bomb. I would liberate the whole of Africa from corruption, fear, terror, detention and death. I would rule the world, alone with nobody. Then invite two Chinese peasants. Only two. A husband and a wife.

In the morning it was three days to Christmas when this woman of a doctor came to my bed and taking my temperature told me to follow her. I looked silly and just like a banyan or a Vietamese in this baby-wool outfit. This pyjama suit striped red and blue, and barefoot. On her tail I looked at her dancing mountains. Shit. Then in this room and from a drawer she pulled out my clothing that I had completely forgotten about. She counted out thirty-six shillings and handed it to me. I asked who the hell it all belonged to? Your money, she said. I said nothing more. Then . . . you are going home today, she told me. I didn't hear her well. What? I asked. You are going home today, she repeated. Saying nothing more she wished me a happy Christmas and New Year. Thank you, I said. And Happy Christmas and New Year. I boarded the route torty bus, heading home. I wanted to reach home and save it. Save that paper of a certificate in that home.

At Katanga tears rolled down my cheeks. The news was that and only that with proof in the newspapers: 'City pulls out the wrecks from Majengo taxi stand'. And no wonder. The car chained to a breakdown truck in the picture was the white Zephyr, the cream of our homes. And worse, with my certificate in it. I cried, for all my hope was completely gone.

I crossed the road without caring about anything. Not even the buses that ran at a high speed when entering the stage. I heard nothing, not even the honking cars. One thing stood in my mind. It was only one thing. I knew death would not come easy at this hour. I didn't want to die. Only one thing stood firmly in my head. I was tired of running away all the time from the law. I was tired of washing cars. I was tired of sleeping in the car with no security. I was tired of the cold and I was tired of the rain. I needed security. Yes, security. And at any cost, right now that was what I needed. I had run away from it but now I thought of it as the only thing and a good thing. Whenever we saw the police we ran away. We avoided the place. But right now it was the only place for me. I could have security, I could have food and I could have the white uniform. But the main thing was the security. The law would take care of me. They would watch me night and day while I worked and slept. No more running. No more. The jail stood in my mind. I was going to be there for whatever length of time the judge would give me. I was going to be there while waiting for the things and time. Things would change in a matter of time, and if I didn't die there I would come out after serving and be a good man. That was now my hope. It was my only hope. My main hope got taken in that wreck of a car. What else had I remaining but to be the government's property? It would feed me and it would clothe me. It would take care of me.

At the taxi-stand the drivers wished me a prosperous long life. They all congratulated me for having escaped death after the kombi plunged into the river. But all this landed on a deaf ear. It landed on a lost man with his own thoughts. A man who had nothing in his head but jail, knocking and hammering hard.

Walking on, I met Hussein seated under a tree, his chin resting on his palms. He was in a lost world just like me. I came to sit beside him before he recognised me. I was thin. We sat, neither asking the other any question. We perhaps all had one thought perhaps. Where to from here? I left him to think of his plan while I thought about mine. What I had was a plan of how I would do it and get a long sentence. I wanted a long sentence from the judge that would keep me far from this place, far from this lost city with all its bastards, women, miraa, two-shilling prostitutes, and far from bhang and cham. Yes, changaa. I wanted to be there and whatever would happen when I came out my future god would know. I wanted that long sentence. That fourteen years, and with strokes perhaps. I didn't want to hear anything. I didn't want to curse any more. I have done that and wished all the evils on the good politicians and all the corrupted living souls. I didn't want to do any more denunciations. For even the Idd went past me without my enjoying it. I knew the free world was for those who felt better. The world, this world, was not for me. Not for poor kind of people like me. To hell with my scattered family. To hell with everyone. My world was my own. I was born once, to suffer and then die. Die when my day came. I thought of how I would do it. I thought of how I would rob with violence, for that was the only good certificate for getting in there, and for the long term. I didn't mind about anybody. I didn't mind about the boys. We were all scattered, each with his own what-to-do-next. That didn't worry me.

I left Hussein sitting and walked around looking for a small piece of iron bar. That would be enough. A small tap on the head of a driver and then run towards the police station. I didn't want the public justice. That mob justice was far from my thinking.

Like God knew, or perhaps understood my feelings, I found one with dust on it. It was long enough.

I came back and found Hussein awake from his dream world.

I sat down and said nothing. I thought of the driver of the milk lorry who took milk in the afternoon to Shauri Moyo shopping centre for the hotel owners' shops. They usually gave him money. Once I attacked that driver and hit him, I would take only a small

180

amount as an exhibit, drop the iron bar and run towards Shauri Moyo Police Station.

Let them shout *Huyo! Huyo! Mwizi! Mwizi!* Thief! Thief! The police would save me from the mob justice. With my plan all complete, Hussein asked me what the iron bar was for? I looked at it and hit the ground hard, sending dust up. I looked at him and said nothing. He asked again, What is it for?

For a robbery, I said.

What do you mean? he asked.

I mean robbery. I am going to kill someone, I said. Want to join me?

I don't understand you, he answered.

What else is there for us? I asked. Our homes are all gone, we are now nothing but vagrants, what else is there for us?

He looked at me and said nothing.

I will rob with violence, run to Shauri Moyo Police Station after hitting the man and wait for the judgement, and of course I will get the long one as an example not to steal again when I leave the prison. And of course you know how it is nowadays, I mean the sentence for that kind of crime, I explained. The government will take care of me and that is not my worry. I will worry the day I come out, if ever I do. Fourteen or seven or ten, with strokes, is not all that bad. It will be a good change for me, I explained.

He looked at me and still said nothing. Do you want to eat? I asked him. Of course it is my last eating with you. It will be my last supper with you, for tomorrow you won't be with me again. I have money and we can eat and drink for the last time, buy a woman for the last time and do anything today for the last time, I said. He looked gloomily at me and said nothing. He shook his head instead. I got up and picked up my iron bar. I am having my walk in the Slums for the last time. Wait for me at the station tomorrow to prove all this I am telling you now.

I walked away with my iron, leaving him seated. The wind blew and the dust covered me.

The new day came. In the afternoon, after seeing Katanga Base for the last time, I walked towards Shauri Moyo for my task. I was determined to do only that. Jail would be my new home.

At Shauri Moyo I didn't have to wait long before the driver pulled his lorry to a stop. I gave him time to collect just a few notes before I hit him with the iron bar, dropped it, took some money and ran towards the station fast, while behind me stones followed, with shouts of Thief! Thief! *Mwizi! Mwizi!*